JOANIE PATYK

Cornflake Gone Clucky

First edition

Editing by Laura Edge
Cover art by Jeannie Talarico

This book was professionally typeset on Reedsy.
Find out more at reedsy.com

In Loving Memory

Rick Patyk
2/22/56-5/12/22

Love suffers long and is kind; love does not envy; love does not parade itself, is not puffed up; does not behave rudely, does not seek its own, is not provoked, thinks no evil; does not rejoice in iniquity, but rejoices in the truth; bears all things, believes all things, hopes all things, endures all things. Love never fails.

1 Corinthians 4-8

Contents

Acknowledgement   ii

1   Brooding Brooders!   1

2   Backyard Life   11

3   Chickens Can Swim!   19

4   Fowl Play   25

5   River Rescue   33

6   Flock Party   42

7   Bathing Beauty   48

8   The Visitor   66

9   Duckling Debut   78

10   Green Pastures   90

11   Cornflake's Homecoming   100

12   Fall Flurries   112

13   Too Many Moms   118

14   Out of the Blue   131

15   The Mystery   143

Epilogue   152

Acknowledgement

A big thank you for your hard work and giving your precious time to make this book a reality. I couldn't have done it without you!

Laura Edge-Copy Editor: reedsy.com

Jeannie Talarico- Book Cover Illustrator: Copyright 2022 All rights reserved. Used with permission. www.facebook.com/-groups/jetspetstudios/

Beta Readers:

- Judy Rupersburg (AKA Mom)
- Faye Hembling
- Marie Patyk

and of course I want to give a shout out to my feathered pets Cornflake, Butterscotch, Penelope, Jellybean, Rhubarb, Dumplin, Cookie, Twinkie, Tickle and Pancake. If only you knew the story I hatched about you! You have been a joy and have taught me much about my Creator to Whom I also give credit for the inspiration to write this novel. My thanks again to all of you!

1

Brooding Brooders!

Bathroom Babies

Nancy Jo beamed from ear to ear as she exited the local farm supply store with a cardboard pet carrier in each hand. She was bringing home four new baby chicks and two new baby ducklings! She bought two chicks each of two different breeds. Two were a breed with an odd name, ISA Brown. The other two chicks were a Leghorn breed.

She chose names for the fuzzy chicks before she even left the store! Nancy Jo chose the names Cornflake and Butterscotch for the two ISA Browns and for the two fluffy Leghorn chicks, she picked the names, Penelope and Jellybean.

In the other pet carrier were the Pekin ducklings which she named Tickle and Twinkie. The baby ducklings were a golden yellow color with bright orange legs and bills. They were so soft to touch! As she carried the tiny Tickle and even tinier Twinkie, the curious Pekin ducklings wondered where they were going. Tickle's round eye peered out the round peephole inside the box.

Spilling over with joy, Nancy Jo cautiously placed the pet carriers in the center of a tire in the back of her dad's pickup, and they drove the itsy-bitsy flock towards a rural area in Turtle County.

Thirty five minutes later they pulled into the country estate wherein sat Cork Pine Cottage which was owned for generations by Nancy Jo's late mother's family. Smoke billowed from the chimney of the charming, rustic stone cottage that Nancy Jo shared with her widower father, Ranger Rick Kimball, and her older brother Cal.

Nancy Jo was still adjusting to life without her sweet mom, Lila Kimball. Little by little Nancy Jo was starting to spring back to life after mourning the crushing loss of her mom, who suffered with a terminal illness for many years until she was taken from her, Cal, and her dad too soon.

Nancy Jo had just celebrated a birthday and had been busy snapping pictures with the new instant Polaroid camera Ranger gave her as a birthday present. She was thirteen and had her whole life of in front of her. She had promised her mom she would try very hard to "turn lemons into lemonade" as her mom put it, though it was easier said than done.

Nancy Jo's bright eyes showed determination and spunk. She

was an active junior member in 4-H Club and now that she was an official teenager, she was old enough to do volunteer work at the senior center on Saturdays! She was even learning how to cook, though her true passion was baking. She had a flair for baking up mouthwatering cakes and cookies, which also helped to satisfy her enormous sweet tooth!

The quiet, secluded cottage sat on a hilltop overlooking a lazy river that attracted many bald eagles that dove for fish. Families of snapping turtles could be seen sunning themselves on Turtle Rock, a rock in the middle of the river that Ranger had nicknamed. Framed within a natural woodsy setting, the quaint cottage offered a peaceful retreat away from noisy city life. The estate was a habitat for plentiful wildlife, and the trees were filled to the brim with the calming sound of chirping birds.

In a flutter of enthusiasm, Nancy Jo briskly carried the pet carriers inside the country estate into the cottage's roomy bathroom. The bathroom would be the chicks' and ducklings' temporary home until they were old enough to live outside.

"Welcome to the baby nursery," said Nancy Jo as she set the carriers down on the floor.

Then she ran out to the garage and returned with two extra roomy Rubbermaid totes which she would use as brooder boxes. She filled the brooder boxes with a thick layer of fresh pine shavings then carefully placed the baby chicks in one box and the ducklings in the other one.

Nancy Jo clamped a heat lamp tightly to the side of one of the boxes careful to keep the hot bulb at a safe distance. The new pets snuggled under the toasty heat lamp. The baby chicken sisters clumped together in their brooder, peeping innocently, and the ducklings huddled together in the corner of their brooder in a lump.

Aah! Such delicate newborns only a few days old, so alert and yet so fragile. As Nancy Jo was admiring her perfect teeny tiny flock, Cal walked in.

"You're keeping livestock in the bathroom? You're nuts, Nancy Jo!"

"It's just until they get their adult feathers!" Nancy Jo fired back.

Cal wasn't impressed; he wasn't an animal lover like Nancy Jo. He only cared about baseball and fishing. Cal was smart, got excellent grades, and played the drums in the Chippewa Junior High marching band. He was a year older than Nancy Jo, but he mostly kept to himself and did what brothers do.

Nancy Jo was thrilled to have a mini farm in her bathroom! She had never raised chickens and ducks before, and she loved most all animals except of course, reptiles and spiders. The pampered pets sensed Nancy Jo's genuine care for them and warmed up to her and loved for her to hold them. Cornflake especially loved all the babying and fussing Nancy Jo made over her. It made her feel cherished.

Tickle and Twinkie

Nancy Jo pulled a faded blue sweatshirt hoodie over her head and brushed her long fine sandy blonde hair in the bathroom mirror, twisting it up into a messy topknot. She didn't like messing with her hair too much and liked it out of the way. Her simple casual style was comfortable, though she did like to experiment with different makeup looks from time to time just for fun. Most of the time she enhanced her blue eyes with a quick flick of mascara and brightened up her fair complexion with a glide of sheer pink lip gloss.

"I will move all of you to the backyard as soon as you're old enough," Nancy Jo promised the flock.

But the fledgling flock was happy in their bathroom home and easy to please, at least at first. The innocent flock had a comfortable start in life and enjoyed plentiful food, fresh water, and fragrant pine shavings to sleep on. However, in a matter of a couple of short weeks everything began to change.

The baby chicks grew some patchy feathers and the gawky ducklings were growing like a pair of gangling tweens! The chicks and ducklings grew incredibly fast and as they grew, their faint chirps and peeps grew louder too. Much to Nancy Jo's surprise, Twinkie got her quack! She was early for her age and quack she did! Her new quack was extra noisy.

"Your duck is giving me a headache!" Cal complained to Nancy Jo. "Can't you make her shut up?"

"I'll try," said Nancy Jo. "Maybe if I close the bathroom door it will help."

Nancy Jo walked into the bathroom and shut the door behind her. She was sure Twinkie was giving her flock mates a headache too.

Twinkie continued, "QUACK, QUACK, QUACK!" Then she belted out boisterously, "I'M GETTING BORED!"

Nancy Jo wanted to keep Twinkie quiet and had an idea. It was time to teach Tickle and Twinkie how to swim! She filled the bathtub with warm water and then set the pair afloat. At once they bobbed in the water and dunked their heads, swimming and splashing water everywhere. In an instant, swimming became their favorite thing to do!

So, every morning when Nancy Jo came to clean the little

flock's brooder boxes the ducks swam in the bathtub while she emptied the soiled, soggy bedding in the boxes and refilled them with fresh fragrant pine shavings. Today Tickle and Twinkie learned how to swim underwater!

After a super energetic romp in the tub, Tickle and Twinkie started to feel drowsy and collapsed on the soft pillowy shavings to rest. Before long they drifted off into a deep, restful slumber. As the weeks passed, Nancy Jo was amazed at how fast the baby chicks and ducklings were growing. Tickle and Twinkie shot up so tall that their heads towered above their brooder box! The chicken sisters had a growth spurt too. More fluffy new feathers grew in, and they doubled in size!

As the flock grew larger, the brooder boxes seemed like they were shrinking in size. Feeling a bit cramped and with the lingering odor from the messy ducks hanging heavy in the air, usually sweet-tempered Cornflake grew uneasy. She had been waiting, quite meekly, for the grand event, when Nancy Jo would move them outside to the backyard. But her patience was wearing thin. She longed to get a glimpse of the backyard hen house, and she was pretty sure it would smell better too. Right now, she only wished she had a nose plug!

Jellybean surprised Nancy Jo when she jumped clear out of her brooder box. She was tired of feeling squished! She was ready for adventure! Jellybean and Penelope were almost identical in appearance except Jellybean was more outgoing and sported an extra- large red floppy comb. Easygoing Penelope, who was more mild-mannered, was starting to lose her cool too. The whole rookie flock grew more restless and impatient with each day.

The next morning the hens were awakened to a strong smell wafting up their beaks. It was a beak curling stench!

"Those smelly ducks!" cried Cornflake.

"Pee-YEW!" Twinkie giggled to herself, knowing she smelled at least some of the time. Okay, maybe she smelled a little more often than that, but she knew she smelled fresh right after her daily dip in the tub. Being smelly was not something that bothered Twinkie in the least. Ducks don't worry about stuff like that.

Twinkie worried more about being entertained with food and drink, and she was easily bored. It didn't take long for Twinkie to have her fill of bathroom living. She wanted more out of life, and she started to protest. Loudly! Her constant and irritating bellyaching was brewing trouble with her flock mates.

"QUACK, QUACK, QUACK!" blasted Twinkie at full volume. "I wanna go outside and see the backyard!" She continued to fuss.

Now annoyed, Butterscotch angrily clucked at her, "Will you button your beak already?"

Twinkie immediately buttoned her beak and quieted down. She had learned to listen to Butterscotch since Butterscotch was the top chicken. Butterscotch was strong, wise and pleasantly plump. The others respected her bossy personality and sensible leadership, even *"Stinky Twinkie."*

Later that morning, Nancy Jo came bursting in to check on her blossoming flock. She noticed the familiar smell and sprayed a heavy fog of Lysol. As she started filling the feeders and waterers, she began singing off key, but her babies didn't care. Her bathroom flock loved when she sang to them! Nancy Jo rolled up the sleeves of her flannel shirt and began the daily unpleasant chore of cleaning out the brooder boxes. Singing silly songs as she worked was Nancy Jo's secret to keeping her

9

sunny side up!

The part Nancy Jo did enjoy was filling up the tub for Tickle and Twinkie. As the water filled the tub, Nancy Jo talked to the bathroom brood.

"All my babies are so big now," she said with a slight whimper in her voice. "I guess it's time to move all of you to the backyard."

The eager flock now buzzed with excitement! "We're moving outside! We're moving OUTSIDE!"

Nancy Jo lovingly watched as she let Tickle and Twinkie take their last swim in the bathtub. After a refreshing swim, Nancy Jo towel dried the squeaky-clean ducklings and loaded them into a massive metal dog crate.

She lugged the bulky crate through a narrow hallway and down a staircase that led to a cozy sitting room. The sunny room had a massive window as well as a sliding glass door. Through the glass the ducks could see the backyard. There were huge trees, green grass, and a winding river softly flowed in the distance. Nancy Jo carried the crate outside and set it atop a grassy hill. When she opened the door, out popped Tickle and Twinkie! The outside world was bright and beautiful to them. Spring was finally here. The sky was deep blue, and the two frisky ducklings were ready to play!

2

Backyard Life

Clyde

Tickle and Twinkie saw Nancy Jo's house cats, Gemma and

Clyde, lounging on lawn furniture. Then their eyes zoned in on two adult ducks in the yard swimming in a kiddie pool. Nancy Jo was duck sitting the two adult ducks for her 4-H friend while she was away on a family vacation. Wanting to join in on the fun Tickle asked the ducks,

"Can we swim in the pool?"

The ducks crabbily quacked back at him and chased Tickle away. The ducklings appeared tiny next to the adult ducks, and they were afraid. Then the oversized drake pushed Tickle down, bit him, and pulled out a chunk of his new feathers.

Nancy Jo stepped in and separated the ducklings from the mean pair with a makeshift chicken wire fence.

"I guess we won't be swimming with the big ducks," said Tickle, but Twinkie didn't hear him because she was too busy poking her bill into the luscious soft mud and slurping up delicious grubs. Tickle and Twinkie forgot all about the other ducks as they played, slurped in the mud, and gobbled up fresh tasty grass.

Soon, Tickle felt sleepy and fell asleep next to the chicken wire fence. He received a rude reminder by the mean drake that they were not welcome. That big bully drake poked his bill through the chicken wire fence, chomped down on Tickle, and pulled out a mouthful of feathers.

Startled, Tickle let out a blood-curdling scream. Feeling unsteady on his legs, he wobbled away from the fence and rested on a soft pile of dirt.

In the meantime, Nancy Jo gathered up the hens one by one, placed them in the metal crate, and then lugged the chicken sisters down to the backyard. The hens' eyes widened with wonder as they took in the wild landscape. A river sparkled in the sunshine and the surrounding thick woods called to them like an invitation for adventure! They could hear the happy songs of birds, and the fresh breezy air lightly ruffled up their feathers.

When they caught a glimpse of the delightful hen house they scurried over for closer inspection. The hen house was spacious enough for all the chickens as well as the ducks. Inside, Tickle and Twinkie had claimed the lower level and were enjoying a nap on the dirt floor. There was also an upper roost area with a narrow ramp leading up to it. The eager hens walked up the ramp into the cozy roost, delighted to discover the floor was deeply cushioned with delicious smelling pine shavings. The happy hens playfully kicked the shavings into the air. Butterscotch, Cornflake, Penelope and Jellybean immediately felt at home in their comfortable roost inside their very own hen house.

After the cloud of pine shavings settled, they sank into the deep bedding of their new home. Cornflake, too silly to sit still, jumped to her feet with an air of confidence. She began to strut her stuff and squawked out a jubilant cheer. At the top of her lungs, she belted out, "We are HENS! We're NOT MEN! This is our H-E-N HEN HOUSE!"

The chicken sisters followed Cornflake's lead and chanted the cheer with gusto! Joining wings, the hens formed a line and kicked their short legs into the air on the word "house." It was a great day to be a hen in the backyard at Cork Pine Cottage!

At last, the exuberant hens wound down, and their high energy soon faded into quiet contentment. The satisfied hens relished their new "big girl" home. Basking in the moment, the only noise they heard was Twinkie's snoring from below—even high-strung Twinkie was calm. The happy hens postponed their backyard adventures and lingered in their new roost. The backyard could wait a little while longer. Grateful for their own hen house and restfully peaceful, they snuggled down deep into the thick pine shavings for a replenishing sister siesta.

The happy mixed flock easily adapted to their new lives in the backyard. The mean adult ducks were still mean, and Tickle was missing a lot of feathers. Nancy Jo was relieved to send the mean ducks back home with her friend upon returning from vacation. At last, Tickle and Twinkie could live in peace.

After that, in blissful freedom, the carefree flock played hard all day in the open meadows. Cornflake, Butterscotch, Penelope and Jellybean played Hide-and-Seek in the woods and foraged in the tender, spring grass. As they stopped to enjoy a dusty roll in a premium pile of dry dirt, Butterscotch snatched up an enormous crunchy bug. It was so fat half of it hung out of her beak! Not wanting to share with her chicken sisters, Butterscotch ran as her sisters chased her for a taste. She managed to gulp down the whole bug before her sisters caught her!

Tickle and Twinkie, after gorging on a massive feast of juicy grubs, made a bee line for the pool. Now it was all theirs to enjoy! They waddled up to the edge of the kiddie pool and dunked just their bills into the cool water. Then they decided to jump in. They splashed and swam as much as their full stomachs would allow, but feeling overstuffed from their heavy meal, their playful pep soon deflated and left them feeling like two shriveled up balloons.

With groggy eyes, Tickle and Twinkie hardly had the energy to even float in the pool until Nancy Jo jolted them with a powerful squirt from the garden hose. The sleepy ducks stumbled out of the pool lickety-split and ran from the stream of water.

"Why are you running from water?" Nancy Jo laughed, poking fun at them. "You're ducks!"

Tickle and Twinkie took a minute to think about that. Tickle agreed and ran back into the spray of water. "I *am* a duck!" he quacked triumphantly as he let the water bounce off his water repellent chest.

Twinkie fully convinced she was a duck too waddled back into the spray. She discovered she loved the invigorating feeling of the water trickling down her feathers. Once Tickle and Twinkie took a liking to the hose, they wanted to be blasted with refreshing squirt sessions all day long!

After a long fun-filled day of playing in the fresh backyard air, Cornflake, Penelope and Jellybean didn't seem to notice that the sun was starting to set, but Butterscotch did. "We better get home," she ordered as the eerie sound of howling coyotes reached her ears.

Cornflake, Penelope and Jellybean followed Butterscotch back to the hen house where Tickle and Twinkie were sleeping on the dirt floor. The dozy hens tiptoed up the narrow ramp to their homey roost for the night as Nancy Jo came outside. Every night at dusk Nancy Jo locked the doors to the hen house to protect the innocent flock from roaming animals that prowled at night, in particular, Vixen, a slinky red fox with an unsavory reputation. Her shrill, ear-piercing screams could sometimes be heard in the nearby woods after dark.

Gemma and Clyde

Several weeks passed. Cornflake, Butterscotch, Penelope and Jellybean began to lay fresh eggs every morning. The proud hens would boastfully announce their daily eggs with loud, joyful squawks.

Cornflake was noticeably fond of her own eggs as well as all of her sister's eggs. When Nancy Jo picked up Cornflake, she noticed her bare stomach. She had plucked out her own belly feathers and her bald skin felt like a warm oven.

As soon as Nancy Jo left the backyard, Cornflake gathered *all* of the fresh eggs under her wings which included her sisters' eggs as well as her own. She rested her warm belly on top of them. As Cornflake lay atop the eggs, she felt like she belonged there. She sat a while and had a striking realization, a divine revelation. It had come to her as if she was hit by a thunderbolt! Cornflake suddenly knew her lifelong purpose, her life's calling. Coming from deep within herself, she had a knowing in her know-er: she wanted to be a mom! She just *knew* this was her purpose!

"Why are you sitting on those eggs?" asked Butterscotch.

"I want to be a mom!" blurted Cornflake.

Butterscotch shook her head. "Cornflake, you can't become a mom. There are no male roosters here to fertilize your eggs. Those eggs you're sitting on will never hatch."

Cornflake didn't understand and persistently lay on the small clutch of eggs.

Twinkie, now a full-grown duck began laying a huge egg every morning too. She saved up a pile of eggs and hid them under the pine shavings. Later, when Nancy Jo came outside Twinkie sat prettily on top of her eggs.

"Quack, quack, quack!" Twinkie beamed with pride. But as

soon as Nancy Jo was gone from the backyard, she forgot all about her eggs and went swimming instead. Maybe she didn't know she would have to sit on the eggs a very long time to hatch baby ducklings. She didn't care about being a mom at all! She only wanted to play!

Cornflake miserably watched as Twinkie waddled off and left her nest of eggs in a sad lonely pile. In the meantime, Cornflake refused to leave her eggs.

"Why are you still sitting on those eggs?" asked Penelope. "You heard Butterscotch. Those eggs will never hatch."

"Yeah," piped in Jellybean. "Listen to Butterscotch!"

Cornflake stubbornly sat on her eggs. She knew her eggs would hatch someday even if her sisters didn't seem to think so. Butterscotch, Penelope and Jellybean rushed off to play Hide-and-Seek in the thick woods leaving Cornflake to sit alone all day on her eggs. She sat, sat and sat some more. Before long she could hear crickets chirp and the flicker of fireflies lit up the evening sky. Soon, the whole flock was back in the hen house for the night. There in the soft glowing moonlight sat Cornflake on her eggs. She didn't care what her other flock mates thought. She knew her unique purpose, and she was not going to let the others steal her dream of becoming a mom. Getting sleepy, she closed her droopy eyelids and had sweet dreams of fuzzy baby chicks huddled under her wings.

3

Chickens Can Swim!

Cornflake

It all happened so fast! Cornflake decided to take a much-deserved break from sitting on her eggs and joined her fluffy chicken sisters in the backyard. Diligently scratching around the backyard, using their feet, the sisters scraped the ground as they scuffled along the edge of the woods.

Twinkie the duck and her handsome mate Tickle were out in the yard too, basking under the cool shade of a voluptuous weeping willow tree. Without warning, Vixen the clever fox, tiptoed out from the edge of the woods and bounded towards them with a wild glint in her eyes and the fierce face of a skilled huntress zeroing in on its prey.

Vixen smacked her lips as she closed in on the flock. "I do love a chicken dinner with all the fix-ins!" she threatened.

The little mixed flock ran in all directions to save their lives. Butterscotch only got a few feet away when Vixen clenched her tail feathers with her sharp teeth. But Butterscotch, being extra robust, was able to wriggle herself free. Cornflake was so afraid she jumped into the river. She rapidly swam away like an athletic, turbo-charged hen!

Cornflake made it halfway across the river and stopped to catch her breath. She glanced back as Vixen stood leering at her from the river bank. Not in the mood for a swim, Vixen gave up her chase and ran after the others.

While in the cottage baking cookies, Nancy Jo's ears tuned in to the noisy bustle coming from the backyard. As she heard the flock's loud distressed squawks, her oven timer went off. Wearing an oven mitt, she pulled out her tray of hot chocolate chip cookies. Then she abandoned them on the kitchen counter, ran outside, and screamed at the top of her lungs, "Get out of here Vixen! NOW!"

She picked up a piece of firewood and hurled it at Vixen. The startled fox cringed and retreated back into the woods.

By now the little flock was scattered and sunsets artistry painted the sky with fiery red and orange hues. Nancy Jo grabbed a flashlight and started searching for her feathered friends. She found Butterscotch hiding in a thick bush. She was missing her tail feathers, but she was okay. Independent Butterscotch who normally didn't like to be babied, was so shaken up that she didn't complain at all when Nancy Jo carried her back to the hen house. Soon Penelope and Jellybean appeared from out of their hiding places and Nancy Jo scooped them up and set them inside their safe, cozy roost.

Worried, Nancy Jo searched for Cornflake. "C-o-r-n-f-l-a-k-e! C-o-r-n-f-l-a-k-e!" she hollered.

Nancy Jo headed to the front yard and at last she could see a shadowy chicken figure slowly trudging up the long driveway. Cornflake had been hiding in her favorite ditch. Bedraggled, soggy, and frightened, Cornflake felt so relieved when she saw Nancy Jo. She was exhausted and longed for home. All she wanted to do was to plop down in sweet pine shavings and sleep in her snuggly roost.

Nancy Jo was relieved to see Cornflake too. "Cornflake, you're okay!" squealed Nancy Jo. Nancy Jo was very fond of Cornflake. She picked up the soggy hen and carried her inside the little stone cottage. Then she wrapped Cornflake in a warm fluffy towel and held her on her lap in the wooden rocking chair in front of the blazing fireplace.

The warmth of the crackling fire calmed Cornflake and made her feel sleepy. Cornflake's jangled nerves melted away as she rocked back and forth, back and forth. Soon the gentle rocking lulled her into a satisfying, peaceful, sound sleep.

The next day when Cornflake was back in the hen house she returned to her clutch of eggs. She had faith her eggs would hatch and consistently kept herself hunkered down on top of them with her warm belly. The rest of the flock ran to meet Nancy Jo who was shaking a box of Cheerios. That beautiful sound! They ran to Nancy Jo as fast as their little legs could carry them. Oh! How they loved snacks, and the sound of the shaking cereal box was like sweet music to their tiny ears!

All, except Cornflake, rushed off for treats. She had been sitting on her eggs for many days now and Nancy Jo worried about her getting her hopes up and having her dreams of being a mom crushed. Cornflake's heart was profoundly aching for fuzzy baby chicks, and she continued on her life's mission to become a mom.

"Your eggs are only good for breakfast," warned Butterscotch. "You have to give up this crazy idea of becoming a mom and have some fun."

Cornflake didn't believe her eggs were duds, though she did struggle with doubts at times. But she kept them to herself.

Penelope returned to the roost and bluntly clucked at Cornflake, "You missed snack time, and you're still wasting time on those eggs that won't hatch!"

Cornflake tried to ignore her, but she wondered why she hadn't hatched any baby chicks yet. *Why are my eggs so slow to hatch?* she wondered.

Penelope, Jellybean and even Tickle and Twinkie pleaded with Cornflake to listen to the wise advice of Butterscotch since she was the top chicken. Cornflake kept up a brave front with the rest of the flock, but she had to admit, at least to herself, her feelings of discouragement were intense at the moment. She couldn't bear the thought that her eggs were only "breakfast eggs" and would never hatch.

Eventually the others left Cornflake alone with her eggs, and big tears rolled down her cheeks. After she had a good cry, she bowed her little head and prayed to God for fuzzy babies. Then she mustered all her strength and told herself, "I'm not giving up! I will hatch fuzzy baby chicks. I will be a mom!"

Early the next morning Nancy Jo came down to the backyard. She shook the Cheerios box as she opened the door to the hen house. As if they were practicing a fire drill, the hens orderly exited in single file down the narrow ramp and Tickle and Twinkie came right behind them ready for delicious Cheerios. The whole flock was always starving and thirsty first thing in the morning but mainly Twinkie. She inhaled food like a powerful vacuum cleaner. She frantically shoveled food in her bill like she'd never eaten before, and it was obvious she didn't care about proper table manners.

Sweet Tickle was such a polite fellow, though sure, he loved Cheerios too, but he made sure Twinkie had her fill first. He was such a gentle drake and so tenderhearted towards Twinkie.

When Twinkie finished her Cheerios, she paused for a long drink to wash it all down. As she drank thirstily, she noticed Tickle watching her with a sweet love-struck sparkle in his eyes. It made her blush. In that rare moment when she wasn't thinking about herself, Twinkie realized her deep feelings for Tickle. She also admired Tickle's striking good looks and quiet strength.

Happy and Free

The pair finished their leisurely breakfast and waddled straight to their kiddie pool. The two ducks, always together, were stuck like muck, enjoying each other's company.

After their swim they nonchalantly waddled away and wandered to a nearby meadow Twinkie picked out, to rest and hatch her daily egg. They savored their freedom to roam the wild acres within the backyard of the country estate. They were happy and free.

4

Fowl Play

Jellybean and Clyde

Penelope and Jellybean paired off from the others. At a distance the white Leghorns looked like twins, but up close you couldn't miss Jellybean's floppy red comb. It drooped down on one side like a stylish hat. The sisters scuffled about in the woods for a bit but then decided to hang out in front of the glass sliding door at the back the cottage. They pressed their beaks up to the glass hoping they would catch a glimpse of Nancy Jo but no such luck. So, they wandered over to the other side of the cottage where they made a surprise discovery. New territory with premium dirt for dust bathing!

"Last one in is a rotten egg!" squawked Jellybean.

Penelope immediately stopped, dropped, and rolled in the rich, savory dirt. She relished indulging herself in a little pampering. After all, a hen needed to look and feel her best. They dug shallow ditches and plunged their bodies deep into the decadent dirt, careful to cover all of their feathers. They even made sure to wash behind their ear lobes.

"I'm squeaky clean!" said Jellybean.

"My feathers are dazzling white!" boasted Penelope. The lavish dust bath was just what they needed!

They met up with Butterscotch who was busy pecking away at something. The sisters were unsure what it was, but it was very satisfying to peck at and it crumbled into teeny tiny pieces with every bite. Whatever it was, it was crunchy and fun to nibble! Ranger, who was mowing the grass, stopped what he was doing to see what the busy hens were up to.

"That's foam board insulation for insulating my workshop," he explained. "It's *not* something to eat!"

The foam board insulation, now peppered with holes, was ruined and seems to scream "utterly useless" as the crumbly bits covered the ground. Ranger stood there for a moment, stunned at the incredible mess the chicken sisters had made.

The busy hens didn't understand why Ranger's eyebrows were changing. They seemed to knit together before their eyes like two fuzzy caterpillars. Noticing the funny uni-brow forming and sensing Ranger's happy mood had changed, they scurried off to find something else to do.

"Those chickens are getting on my last nerve," Ranger muttered to himself as he cleaned up the mess the silly hens had left behind. Usually even tempered, Ranger knew he was not quite himself. He missed Lila terribly and still wore his wedding ring on his left hand.

Jellybean went to check to see if Nancy Jo had fed her cats yet. She kept a close eye on the outside cat food dish and would eat the cats' leftovers. She didn't care that it was chicken flavored—she loved cat food! She hoped Buttons the raccoon hadn't gotten to it first, as he also regularly patrolled the cat food dish.

This time Jellybean lucked out! After scoring a few tasty morsels she caught up to the others who were enjoying a bug picnic in their favorite secret ditch in the front yard. Jellybean munched on crunchy insects with her sisters in the secret ditch.

Nancy Jo didn't like to see the girls in the front yard because of the nearby road and the occasional speeding car. She said it was "dangerous for chickens" and would shoo them to the backyard if she saw them there. However, the mischievous chicken sisters had a way of getting into everything!

In the meantime, back at the hen house, Cornflake sat on her eggs. She was missing out on all the joys of life outdoors. She only came outside to eat a quick bite and have a few sips of water and then returned to her post. She was starting to look frail and raggedy.

Cornflake worried Nancy Jo as well as the rest of the flock as she spent all her time on top of those eggs. Nancy Jo wondered what she could do to help Cornflake, but she didn't know how to remedy the situation, at least not yet. She knew she had to come up with an idea soon though. She couldn't bear to see Cornflake pining away for baby chicks and looking so dreadfully skinny.

The next morning Ranger yelled out the kitchen window down to the backyard below. "Don't forget your 4-H Club meeting is today."

"OK Dad!" Nancy Jo hollered back. Good thing Ranger had reminded her! She had forgotten all about it.

Nancy Jo threw down a little cracked corn for her flock and hurried into the cottage. She changed out of her chicken print pajama pants and slipped into her favorite jeans. In her closet she found a flowy coral pink tunic blouse with the tags still attached. The loose cotton blouse looked even better on and Nancy Jo felt beautiful in it. She swept up her long hair into a ponytail and applied a creamy peach shade of lipstick. Then she donned a simple pair of silver hoop earrings. Nancy Jo was ready in a flash!

She found Ranger still in the kitchen scrubbing up the sink.

"Wow, you cleaned up nice!" said Ranger, surprised to see her all ready to go.

It was amazing what a change of clothes and a touch of lipstick could do! Nancy Jo's fair complexion had an instant boost of brightness and it felt good to be dressed so she was presentable to the human race instead of just to the chickens and ducks.

Nancy Jo and Ranger arrived at her 4-H meeting just as Miss Marjorie, the vivacious club leader, walked in carrying a small wire crate with a chicken inside. Miss Marjorie Parker was not

28

only the club leader, but she also attended the little country church that Nancy Jo and Ranger went to every Sunday.

"Hi, Miss Marjorie!" said Nancy Jo.

"Well, hello to you too! I brought Gladys with me today."

Gladys was a fluffy white Cochin breed hen with feathered feet. "Did you know this fancy Cochin breed dates back to the 1800s?" asked Miss Marjorie. "Did you know that Queen Victoria herself favored this breed?" Miss Marjorie went on to explain, "The Queen was given a Cochin hen as a gift, and then she fell in love with them!"

Nancy Jo thought Gladys certainly looked gentle and regal. She could see why they were a favorite of the Queen of England.

Ranger and Miss Marjorie exchanged friendly chit chat while Nancy Jo held Gladys and stroked her fluffy feet. As the 4-H club kids poured in Miss Marjorie started the meeting by formally introducing Gladys to the class.

"This is Gladys, and she has won several purple and blue 4-H ribbons at different local fairs. I'm excited to announce that the Turtle County Fair will be here soon. If anyone is interested in chicken showmanship, please see me to enroll in the chicken project after my demonstration."

Miss Marjorie then presented Gladys as if she was showing her before a panel of judges, posing her and showing how to hold her just right. Gladys was so pliable and gentle she could stand alone in a perfect show pose without any help from Miss Marjorie. She was a chicken super model, poised and elegant!

After the demonstration Nancy Jo anxiously signed up to be in the chicken project. Maybe this would be the thing to snap Cornflake out of her nesting box obsession. She couldn't wait to get home and practice with Cornflake, her soon-to-be show chicken!

Jellybean, Tickle and Twinkie

The morning skies were a dreary dull gray. Tickle slowly strolled the wet grass looking for grubs while Twinkie went off to a private grassy spot to lay her egg. Tickle kept a close eye on Twinkie. Like a proud duck soldier, he marched back and forth as if he was Twinkie's personal body guard. He watched over her while she laid her egg in the distance.

As Twinkie's loyal protector, Tickle took his guard duty responsibilities seriously because he was completely smitten with Twinkie. When Twinkie finished laying her egg, the two took a leisurely stroll near the river's edge.

Jellybean scurried to check the cat food dish again while Butterscotch and Penelope scratched and scraped the ground with their feet near the edge of the woods looking for treats from the wet earth.

Nancy Jo topped off the fresh food and water for the flock and was happy to see that Cornflake had left her beloved nest to eat a little something for breakfast. Nancy Jo sang as she finished up her outside chores and noticed several deer watching her from the opposite riverbank. Looking relaxed, they seem to enjoy her singing and were listening attentively. A flock of Canadian Geese quietly floating in the river seem to be listening too. The nearby wildlife had come to know Nancy Jo's familiar voice, and Nancy Jo was stunned as she took notice of her quirky audience of adoring fans!

She finished stuffing the roost with fresh pine shavings and rushed off to her weekend volunteer job at the community senior center where the older folks met for hearty lunches filled with friendly conversations and laughter. After lunch the seniors played bingo for scrumptious prizes donated by the corner bakery. A lucky winner got first pick from the prizes. There were elegant pastries, decorated cakes, cookies and a variety of bakery treats to choose from. The Baked Goods Bingo Game was always a hit and very popular with the locals. The best part was that eventually everyone got to take home a yummy prize at the end because there were always plenty of extra desserts to go around.

As the crowd thinned out, Nancy Jo helped clean up the senior center cafeteria. As she wiped down the long tables, her thoughts returned to Cornflake's problem. She hoped getting Cornflake involved as a show chicken would help to get her one-track mind off her eggs. Nancy Jo was eager to show off her precious Cornflake! She was excited to be a part of the chicken project instead of being in the cake decorating division like she had been for the last two years. Even though she had won ribbons for her decorated creations, she was ready for a change.

Soon, Ranger showed up to give her a ride home, and they headed back to Cork Pine Cottage. She couldn't wait to see her beloved backyard flock! Back home in the cottage kitchen, she pulled a family sized box of Cheerios out of the pantry and headed outside. She shook the box of Cheerios like always, but today things seemed different. Not one of the animals came running to her—not one—and it was peculiarly silent.

She cried out all their names. "Tickle, Twinkie come and get some Cheerios!" "Butterscotch! Cornflake! Jellybean! Penelope! Where are you?"

Puzzled, Nancy Jo began hunting for her beloved flock. She carefully scouted the whole backyard, but they could not be found. Nancy Jo then walked on to check the front yard. There, under a thick cluster of overgrown lilac bushes hidden by greenery, she discovered her frightened hens huddled close together.

Nancy Jo could barely see the chickens under the tangled bushes, so she shook her cereal box and out jumped Butterscotch! Nancy Jo headed back to the hen house with the girls obediently trailing behind her. Once in the backyard Nancy Jo realized Jellybean wasn't with the rest of the group. Her heart sank. Jellybean was still missing!

Nancy Jo rustled Butterscotch, Penelope and Cornflake back inside the hen house and locked the deadbolt. Safe inside, they enjoyed a filling dinner including a treat of heirloom asparagus Nancy Jo picked fresh from the garden. As the girls settled into the hen house for the night, Nancy Jo headed off to search for Tickle, Twinkie and Jellybean.

5

River Rescue

Tickle and Twinkie

Nancy Jo continued to comb the backyard for Tickle, Twinkie and Jellybean. She went down to the river and shook the cereal box.

"Who wants Cheerios?" she called out as she scanned the riverbank.

Then, out of the corner of her eye she caught a glimpse of Twinkie on the other side of the river. She was quacking hysterically at the top of her lungs, and she was obviously shaken up. She answered Nancy Jo loud and clear!

Nancy Jo ran to get her dad. Ranger untied his canoe from a tree near the river's edge and the two lowered the canoe onto a stretch of sandy shoreline. Using the canoe oars, they shoved off the sandy bank and paddled across to the opposite riverbank.

Twinkie was tightly tucked under a low tangled deep thicket of branches. Nancy Jo stooped under the branches, and when she was able to get close enough, she threw an old sheet she had grabbed from home over Twinkie and scooped her up. Once Twinkie was snug in her arms, she pulled the sheet back and uncovered Twinkie's little head.

Twinkie's eyes were wide with fright, and she wiggled in Nancy Jo's arms. The bed sheet kept the sharp claws on Twinkie's webbed feet from digging into Nancy Jo's arms. Twinkie was upset and Nancy Jo didn't want to upset her even more with a bumpy canoe ride home. She also didn't think she could manage boarding the tippy canoe holding a wiggly duck.

Ranger paddled back across the river by himself so he could return on land in his pickup truck. The road that ran behind the bank where Twinkie and Nancy Jo waited would be easier to get to with his truck, and he could drive them both back home.

Nancy Jo held Twinkie tight to her chest, and as the duck continued to wiggle, she wrestled to hang on to her. Poor Twinkie didn't want to be held, she wanted to run. She panted hard as Nancy Jo tried to calm her, but nothing helped. Nancy Jo hoped she could keep a grip on Twinkie until Ranger came back in the truck. Her arms were starting to ache.

After what seemed like an hour, Nancy Jo heard the familiar rumble of Ranger's pickup truck getting closer. "Don't worry, Twinkie! We're going home!" she rejoiced.

Ranger pulled up and stopped. Nancy Jo, with both her arms full holding Twinkie, tried to get into the truck. But the truck sat high off the ground and her arms were full of wiggly duck, so she couldn't get the door open. After a couple clumsy attempts, Ranger realized her struggle and got out of the truck to give Nancy Jo and Twinkie a little dad powered boost into the passenger seat. Nancy Jo sighed a deep sigh of relief as they headed home.

Minutes later, Twinkie arrived back home safe and secure in the hen house. Twinkie was thankful to be in her own backyard, but she soon gave in to worry. Twinkie was troubled as there was still no sign of Tickle or Jellybean. Nancy Jo had searched and searched for them, but sadly, they never turned up.

The remaining hens were quiet for the next several days. Penelope was sad, and they missed their flock mates, Jellybean and Tickle. Twinkie missed Tickle and cried all day and every night. She wailed so loudly nobody could get any sleep.

"I want Tickle!" she cried. Twinkie's heart was broken, and she carried on for days. She couldn't seem to help herself. She was an emotional puddle of tears.

After more than a few sleepless nights Ranger came home with a surprise for Twinkie. "Here you go Twinkie, meet Pancake!" Twinkie's eyes lit up and her heart fluttered with excitement! Ranger bought Pancake from a tiny farm owned by a poor family. Pancake was a polite but skinny drake who appeared under fed. His belly hung loose on his large frame and his white feathers were dirty and tattered. Pancake sheepishly took his place as the newest member of the backyard flock.

Twinkie, fascinated by the enchanting new drake, magically turned on the charm and batted her eyes at him. "Why, hello, handsome!" she flirted. Twinkie didn't waste any time claiming him as her new mate and Pancake didn't have a say in the matter as far as she was concerned. She didn't notice that he was skinny and dirty, Twinkie only saw perfection! In her eyes Pancake was a handsome dreamboat. And he was all hers!

Cookie

The backyard was a lot quieter now that Twinkie had settled down with her new mate. Even the neighbors were enjoying restful sleep once again. Pancake was adjusting to his new life and instant girlfriend Twinkie. Pancake didn't miss a meal and ate generous portions of food like each meal was his last. With his hearty appetite and an abundance of food he soon filled out and transformed into a strong, healthy drake. Twinkie made sure Pancake took extra dips in the kiddie pool too, so his dull dirty feathers were now shiny and bright white.

While Pancake and Twinkie were much happier, Butterscotch, Cornflake and Penelope missed their mischievous sister

Jellybean. There was no replacement for sweet Jellybean, but a kind neighbor who heard that Jellybean went missing offered Nancy Jo an extra hen he had. Nancy Jo accepted the hen and hoped it would lift the chicken sisters' spirits.

"Maybe a new hen will help," Nancy Jo told her neighbor. "They have been down in the dumps."

Nancy Jo introduced the new hen to Butterscotch, Cornflake and Penelope. "This is Cookie!" But they were not interested in a newcomer. Nancy Jo kept Cookie in a dog crate inside the run with the others, so they could gradually get acquainted.

Cookie felt overwhelmed as the new girl, and it hurt her feelings that the others ignored her. Sad and painfully aware of her loneliness, she ate her feelings and stuffed herself with her favorite snack, cracked corn. Cookie couldn't understand why the other hens didn't act friendly to her or why they seemed unimpressed that she could lay beautiful green eggs, something she was very proud of. Feeling sorry for herself she passed the time singing sad melodies. Her favorite gloomy song to sing was called "Nobody Loves Me or my Green Eggs," followed by an encore of indulgent, high calorie snacking.

Butterscotch, Cornflake and Penelope still felt the loss of their sister Jellybean. It was not that they hated Cookie, they just wanted Jellybean back.

Cornflake was still desperately trying to hatch those eggs. She faithfully sat on her eggs and only took short breaks to stretch her legs or to refresh herself with a tidbit of food or water. Nancy Jo's keen, watchful eyes observed Cornflake's faithful devotion and decided it was time to work with Cornflake on her show routine for the fair.

"Cornflake, I think you will make a great show chicken!"

Cornflake rolled her eyes at the thought. "I want to be a mom, not a show chicken!"

Cornflake sighed but Nancy Jo insisted Cornflake do her best "show girl" stance for her. Cornflake certainly needed work. Her head drooped and her slouchy posture made her look more like a rubber chicken than a regal show chicken. Cornflake went through the motions, but her heart wasn't in it. She just wanted practice to be over!

"Nancy Jo!" Ranger hollered down to the backyard. "Mary Kay is on the phone!"

"Okay, Dad, I'll be right there," Nancy Jo shouted back.

Cornflake was happy to be released from her grueling practice routine. She bolted back to her roost like a freed prisoner. It was time to get back to her first order of business, becoming a mom!

After a couple weeks of painstaking chicken posing practice, the exciting day had come. The County Fair was in full swing and it was time to show off Cornflake in the 4-H poultry showmanship contest! Nancy Jo whisked Cornflake up off her nest of eggs and put her into a cat carrier. Cornflake was not at all pleased with being dragged away from her beloved eggs. Sweet Cornflake was being difficult.

"I don't want to be carted off to some stupid fair!" she squawked grumpily. But Nancy Jo, listening to music on her headphones, didn't hear Cornflake's fussing. At the fair Nancy Jo waited for her turn to show Cornflake in front of the judge. She was a little nervous, but she had studied poultry showmanship over the last couple of weeks, and she was confident she could wing it.

"Nancy Jo Kimball," called out the judge. It was her turn! Nancy Jo carried Cornflake to an exhibit cage and the judge asked her several questions about breed, care and different parts of poultry. Nancy Jo aced the questions. Now it was time to position Cornflake to show off her head, eyes, wings, under color of feathers, breast bone, feet and toes.

She removed Cornflake from the exhibit pen and shouldered her to show off her eyes. Cornflake's eyes flashed with anger; she was seething mad. Instead of showing off her noble qualities, she looked like a common broiler breed mixed with evil! As Nancy Jo positioned Cornflake for her final stand-alone pose, Cornflake, still in a snit, refused to pose like some uppity "Miss Priss!" Exasperated, she hunched her shoulders in a most unflattering way and hung her head down. Cornflake was modeling her signature rubber chicken pose again and looked very amateur, but she didn't care.

The judge took notice of Cornflake's sour attitude, unpolished stance and ordinary breed. Then he wrote some notes down on his clipboard. Well, that was it; it was over. Cornflake did not win any ribbons, but Nancy Jo won an award for her outstanding poultry knowledge with a purple ribbon! Cornflake just wanted to go back to Cork Pine Cottage STAT! Her eggs were waiting for her!

Back at the hen house Nancy Jo put her crabby bird back in her roost. Cornflake sighed a huge sigh of relief as she snuggled back into her nest and planted herself on her eggs again. She wasn't the fancy type, and she didn't want to be fancy either.

Cornflake apologized to Nancy Jo. "I'm sorry", she clucked, but I'm just a simple chicken!"

Nancy Jo had to agree. Cornflake was not the ornamental type of chicken. She was not a fancy Silkie or Cochin. She was a more practical type chicken.

Nancy Jo softly stroked Cornflake's feathers. "That's okay, Cornflake. I think you're simply fabulous."

As Cornflake's baby fever was reaching a boiling point Nancy Jo knew she had to do something. When Cornflake jumped up off her eggs to grab a nibble and slurp a few sips of cool water, an idea suddenly popped into Nancy Jo's head. Seizing the moment of opportunity, in the blink of an eye, Nancy Jo secretly removed Cornflake's dud eggs and replaced them with three of Twinkie's fertile eggs!

Cornflake came back to her eggs not knowing her eggs had been swapped. She took her place atop the eggs, careful not to crack them. Cornflake hunkered down and kept them warm with her hot belly. More determined than ever, Cornflake did not budge. She cared more for those eggs than herself, looking even thinner and scragglier as days turned into weeks.

6

Flock Party

Happy Flock

Nancy Jo headed outside to check on her feathered pets.

Pancake and Twinkie greeted her with joyful quacking. Their heads bobbed up and down. They loved Nancy Jo, and they also loved treats! Nancy Jo tossed them some Cheerios and a bit of dry cat food. Then she went to the roost to check in on Cornflake.

Cornflake seemed content just sitting there with her feathers puffed up over her eggs. Nancy Jo noticed something peeking out from underneath her. It was a cracked eggshell! She wondered why there was a broken eggshell, so she lifted up Cornflake's wing and took a peek underneath. When she lifted up Cornflake's wing, she gasped! There was a tiny hatched baby duckling covered with soft baby fuzz! She was excited to find two more newborn ducklings hiding under Cornflake's opposite wing. Thanks to Nancy Jo's quick thinking and Twinkie's eggs, Cornflake had indeed become a mom!

Nancy Jo ran off and returned with her camera. "I'm so proud of you, Cornflake!" she cheered. "Say cheese!"

Cornflake gushed with pride and her heart surged with love for the new babies nestled under her wings. Her impossible dream had come true and her heart was happy and full.

Curious, Butterscotch and Penelope popped in to see the big event. They were surprised her eggs had hatched and were eager to see the babies. They noticed the baby chicks looked a little different, but even so, they were happy for Cornflake. Butterscotch and Penelope boisterously broadcast the news of the triplets' birth to the backyard and all the neighbors with loud crows of joy!

Being cautious with the delicate ducklings Nancy Jo didn't let the noisy hens stay long. She shooed them out and shut the door to the roost so Cornflake and her babies could have it all to themselves for a while. There Cornflake nurtured the babies with tender care and Nancy Jo put a tiny feeder and waterer inside the roost for them.

It was a day of celebration! Nancy Jo blasted Kokomo by The Beach Boys from the patio radio. As the mellow rhythmic sounds streamed through the airwaves, a chill island vibe filled the atmosphere of the familiar backyard. The pleasant melodic tune lifted the spirits of the flock and made them feel as if they were transported to an exotic vacation destination.

Pancake softly swayed his head from side to side to the relaxing beat of the beachy music, Butterscotch and Penelope were in a festive mood too and Butterscotch proposed a toast in honor of the joyous occasion.

"To Cornflake! The new mom! I don't know how you did it, but I'm glad you did!"

Cornflake heard Butterscotch from inside the roost. Her heart swelled and tears welled up and sparkled in her eyes. Then they all guzzled healthy lemon drop mock tails that Nancy Jo made with chilled ice water and fresh squeezed lemon juice. Even gloomy Cookie took a break from her binge eating and got into the swing of the special occasion. Her funk changed to spunk! She felt at long last like she belonged for the first time since she arrived. It was a fabulous blowout bash!

Cornflake

Nancy Jo moved Cornflake and her babies to a roomy dog travel kennel so Cornflake could raise her babies in their own space away from the others. Cornflake was a very good mom to her newborn baby ducklings. She kept them sheltered under her protective wings, and when one of her babies managed to escape, she used her wings to pull them back under her.

The ducklings were very energetic, and even though they loved to snuggle under Cornflake's wings every night, during the daytime, they were playful and liked to climb onto her back and play Hide-and-Seek in her feathers. The ducklings splashed most of the water out of the little waterer. Nancy Jo replaced the almost empty mini waterer with a recycled crock pot that was taking up space in the kitchen. As soon as she put the heavy crock of fresh water inside the kennel, a duckling was floating on top! The drinking water was now a fun mini pool for the baby ducklings.

Although Cornflake was puzzled by her babies' need to swim in their drinking water, she overlooked their unusual behavior because she loved them. They were her babies, and they were perfect! During the day Cornflake showed the ducklings how to find bugs and grubs, using certain clucking sounds to teach them. The cute baby ducklings chirped melodiously as they followed Cornflake wherever she went, and Cornflake never left them alone for one minute.

Ranger and Nancy Jo were busy attaching heavy-duty hardware cloth fencing to fence posts to form a new enclosure for the flock. The new enclosure attached to the hen house so the flock could come and go as they pleased and play in safety.

The new run had a small in ground stock tank pond inside for Twinkie and Pancake to swim in, and an old tire filled with sandy dirt served as a dust bathing station for the hens.

Nancy Jo decided to let Cornflake's babies test out the new in ground pond. As Cornflake neared the entrance to the run, she came face to face with Cookie whom she never really had a chance to properly meet. Cookie was curious about the ducklings and stepped forward to get a closer look, but Cornflake shooed her young behind her and forcefully cackled out a shrill war cry followed by a warning.

"You will not come near my babies!"

Suddenly, Nancy Jo saw a fierce side of Cornflake the likes of which she'd never seen before. Cornflake was like a mighty she warrior aggressively protecting her babies. She jumped in the air like a black belt in karate. Her sharp claws pointed out in all directions like little knives ready to shred poor Cookie to ribbons.

Cookie stood her ground. She sprang into the air and pounced on Cornflake.

"You're not the boss of me!" she screeched.

Nancy Jo managed to separate the two hens before they had a chance to peck each other's eyes out. Nancy Jo put Cookie back in the hen house with the other hens. This gave Cornflake's babies the freedom to take a dip in the pond without worrying about another match of Chicken Kung Fu.

Cornflake doted on the ducklings at the edge of the pond while they swam, dunked their heads, and played tag. Cornflake did not understand why her babies had such a fascination with water. Looking a bit worried she stayed very close as they swam and swam and swam some more!

7

Bathing Beauty

Lady Cornflake
49

Nancy Jo was hustling and bustling inside the cottage rushing to bust through some boring but necessary household chores. She and Ranger were getting ready for company! Nancy Jo's Aunts, Ranger's sisters, Aunt Mimi and Aunt Elaine, and both of her uncles would be visiting along with her three cousins Betsy, Lynette, and Jimbo.

Aunt Elaine and Aunt Mimi were concerned about Ranger since his precious Lily had passed on. Ranger kept himself busy, he said it helped him cope, but his sisters worried he was busy avoiding his grief. There was a definite sadness that still clung to him.

Aunt Mimi was a smart, savvy real estate broker. She was all business on the outside, but on the inside, she was all mush. Her family was always her first priority. Aunt Elaine was a strong-willed, independent woman too who trained horses and ran her own horse farm along with her husband, Uncle Fester. Her hair was very long, strong, and thick like a horse's tail! Their daughter Betsy, Nancy Jo's cousin, inherited Aunt Elaine's bubbly personality and love of horses, but their other son, Jimbo, Nancy Jo's other cousin, was into other things. Jimbo liked to tinker with engines, and like Cal, he loved to fish. He even played the tuba though he didn't seem to realize he was hopelessly tone-deaf.

Ranger was busy cooking a ham supper with homemade potato salad and deviled eggs. Nancy Jo had made a fluffy coconut layer cake the night before as well as a batch of her famous crispy chocolate chip cookies. She was eager to get outside and soak up some sunshine and fresh air on this mild summery day.

The cottage windows facing the backyard hen house were

open and Twinkie and Pancake could hear Nancy Jo moving about. The pair had keen hearing, and even when the windows were latched shut, they would listen closely for Nancy Jo's voice. This would trigger a round of happy duck quacking. Twinkie was, of course, very vocal and boisterous, and Pancake's softer raspy quack sounded like he had a case of duck laryngitis.

Nancy Jo finished her chores and ran outside to fill a new camouflage-patterned kiddie pool that Ranger had picked up for Cornflake's baby ducklings. Now they had a pool all to themselves!

Butterscotch, Penelope and Cookie gawked from inside the enclosed run as Cornflake and the ducklings casually dilly-dallied around the outside perimeter of the run, pecking the ground for whatever tasted good. By now it was obvious that Cornflake's babies were not chickens. The baby ducklings had grown big and tall!

Just waking up from her third nap of the day, Twinkie lazily lifted her head and got a quick glimpse of Cornflake with her babies trailing behind her in a perfect line. Looking stunned, she stumbled to her feet. Her eyes widened as they zoomed in on the ducklings. Twinkie waddled closer to the mesh fencing and studied the ducklings with her head cocked to one side and with a quizzical look on her face.

She stared long and hard at them. They seemed oddly familiar to her, but she didn't know why. She noticed something was different about them too; they didn't look a bit like Cornflake!

Twinkie did not realize that she was the actual biological mother to the ducklings or that Nancy Jo had swapped out Cornflake's eggs and replaced them with *her* eggs for Cornflake to hatch. Suddenly distracted by a slight growl in her stomach, Twinkie didn't give another thought to the ducklings and waddled off for a post lunch snack.

As soon as Nancy Jo topped off the kiddie pool, the three baby ducklings waddled over. The sparkling, fresh pool water was inviting, and they couldn't resist taking a dip. In they went as Cornflake hugged the outside edge of the pool. She monitored them like a trained lifeguard. Her mother hen instinct was strong, and her love for them was even stronger. With all the water splashing around from the little pool, the ground soon became muddy. Cornflake's legs looked like she was wearing socks! Mud socks! Cornflake didn't seem to mind wearing mud socks up past her ankles though. She was too busy being a mom to care. She did, however, wonder why her baby chicks loved to swim, yet she wholeheartedly loved them with unconditional love. The ducklings loved their mom too. They didn't even notice that their mom was a chicken. She was the best mom a duckling could ever have!

Lifeguard Mom
53

"Hi, Nancy Jo!"

Nancy Jo turned around to see her two cousins, Betsy and Lynette, in the backyard. "You're here!" she exclaimed as she rushed over to greet them with hugs. "How are my little cousins?"

Both girls, spilling over with youthful pep, were admiring Nancy Jo's flock from outside the run. Even though her cousins were close in age to Nancy Jo, she dubbed them her *little* cousins.

Elizabeth, who went by Betsy for short, was twelve and full of spice. She spouted back to Nancy Jo, "Howdy, country cousin! You're such a hick, I knew you would be in the backyard!"

As the girls giggled, Lynette noticed Nancy Jo's spectacular long eyelashes. "Wow, your lashes are so long!"

"They're fake," chuckled Nancy Jo. "I can put some on you later if you want."

"Okay!" Lynette agreed heartily, gung-ho to try a trendy new look.

Lynette was a gorgeous girl, inside and out. She was a kind-hearted cat lover and at the tender age of eleven she was already turning into a crazy cat lady! So far, she had rescued five lucky cats from the local animal shelter.

Aunt Mimi, Uncle Anton, Aunt Elaine and Uncle Fester knocked at the front door of the cottage. When Ranger opened the door, they were shocked to see how rail thin he was.

"You need to eat your own cooking!" said Aunt Elaine.

"I'm fine," said Ranger. "I just don't have much of an appetite."

"I know you love cheese, so I made a cheese ball," said Aunt Mimi, shoving a plate of cheese and crackers in front of him within minutes of arriving. "Here, have a taste."

Uncle Fester and Uncle Anton were happy to see their skinny brother-in-law. "I hear you got a new pool table," said Uncle Anton.

"Yup!" said Ranger eager to entertain some willing pool players. "How 'bout a game?"

"I'll play the winner!" piped in Uncle Fester.

Back in the backyard, Nancy Jo turned to the girls. "So, what do you wanna do today?"

"Let's go for a canoe ride down the river!" screeched Lynette in a high pitched voice that could shatter glass. She jumped up and down with girlish glee .

"Or maybe we could go fishing!" shouted Betsy.

Cal and Jimbo were heading towards the river with their fishing poles and overheard the girls as they walked by. Cal interrupted, "I have a better idea! Let's have a fishing contest. Loser has to clean the fish."

Jimbo's face lit up. "Game on, CUZ! Get ready to be blown away! I have mad fishing skills not to mention the latest Fish Whisperer edition rod." Jimbo an overly confident thirteen-year-old, was definitely up for the challenge!

"The girls get the canoe!" yelled Nancy Jo. The three girls scrambled to find fishing poles and then piled into the canoe. Cal grabbed the bow of the canoe and shoved them off the river's edge. The girls headed downstream with their fishing poles and worms.

Cal and Jimbo got started right away. They baited their hooks with fat night crawlers and cast their lines from the river bank. The two were so serious! Cal dug his fish scale out of his tackle box to weigh the fish they caught. "Whoever catches the most weight in fish wins. Starting now," he said in a matter-of- fact voice.

"When does the contest end?" asked Jimbo.

"Oh, how about when Ranger calls us for supper?" answered Cal.

"Okay," said Jimbo. "Let's catch some fish!"

The river was full of many species of fish. It was a fun place to fish and full of surprises. You never knew what you would find on the end of your line.

Nancy Jo, Lynette and Betsy paddled to a quiet spot and stopped to bait their hooks. While they were preoccupied, they didn't notice they were heading straight towards some boulders.

BAM! The canoe hit the boulders head on.

The girls were startled at first but then broke into a fit of giggles. They used their paddles to try to shove off the huge rocks, but the canoe was stuck on a tall rock underneath.

"I guess I'll have to get out and push it off the rocks," said Nancy Jo.

Betsy yelled, "Help us, Hayseed!" and the girls' bellowing laughter echoed down the river.

Very lightly, Nancy Jo swung one leg over the canoe and plopped into the water. She managed to jiggle free the canoe and then stood on top of one of the protruding boulders and nimbly got back into the canoe. She was drenched to the bone and smelled like the river.

Betsy and Lynette couldn't stop laughing. "What's that fancy perfume you're wearing? Filet-O-Fish?" teased Betsy and Lynette as they plugged their noses.

"Want me to flip this canoe?" asked Nancy Jo

"No thank you!" said Betsy as she wriggled her nose, "I don't want to smell like a swamp!"

Jimbo reeled in a whiskered catfish. "She's a beauty!" he

exclaimed. He weighed the catfish on the scale. "Two pounds!"

Shortly after, Cal caught a good size small mouth bass. It weighed three and a half pounds.

"Wow!" said Cal. He put the fish on the stringer, put a fresh fat night crawler on his hook, and cast his line near some rocks. Minutes later, he reeled in a decent rock bass. The fishing contest was growing intense!

The bite was on! Nancy Jo and her cousins tried to focus and get down to business about their fishing too, but with all the racket they made, they must have scared the fish away for miles. They didn't hook a single fish, but they had a jolly good time even so, floating down the river, enjoying the scenic water trail and taking turns paddling.

After a while, the girls decided to give up on their fishing trip. They paddled back to the cottage and threw the anchor onto the river bank where Cal and Jimbo were fishing. Nancy Jo and Lynette exited the tippy canoe. Betsy, not known for being graceful, stood up abruptly and put all her weight on one side of the canoe. The canoe began to tip, and she was very surprised when she suddenly found herself splashing into the river.

The girls howled with laughter and their noise irritated Cal and Jimbo as they were still in the thick of a serious fishing match.

"You're scaring the fish," scolded Jimbo in a whispered tone.

The girls hurried off to find some dry clothes, giggling all the while as they ran uphill towards the cottage. Cal and Jimbo stayed focused and concentrated on their fishing. By now Jimbo had also caught a Sucker, a Red Horse and a Blue Gill. Jimbo added up the weight of all his fish, 6.3 pounds (2.86 kg) in all.

Cal was disappointed when he caught a tiny five-ounce Pumpkin Seed sunfish. Cal added up his fish weight, only 4.3 pounds (1.95 kg). After a half hour of catching nothing, Cal cast his line out near a submerged log when at last he got a bite! Cal tugged the line to set the hook. He could feel it was a good sizer. Excited, he reeled it in to shore.

"I'll net him," said Jimbo. He grabbed the fishing net and scooped out a beautiful Walleye. Just then they heard Ranger ringing the cowbell in the backyard. It was time for supper.

Well, it didn't take much calculating to tally up their fish weights. Jimbo caught 6.3 pounds (2.86 kg) in all and Cal had already caught 4.3 pounds (1.95 kg). Jimbo weighed the Walleye. It was 4 pounds (1.81 kg). Cal won the fishing contest with a grand total of 8.3 pounds (3.76 kg).

"I win!" said Cal. "You get to clean the fish."

"I think the girls should clean the fish," said Jimbo.

"Well, they should, but they don't know how," said Cal.

"Okay, I guess I'm stuck with it," said Jimbo. "I'm getting hungry; let's get some supper." The two grabbed their stringers of fish and headed in.

After a delicious and filling ham supper Nancy Jo carefully applied false eyelashes to her cousins' eyelids. "These will make your eyes pop!" said Nancy Jo.

The girls were so giddy with their new fluttery long lashes, they each did a double take in the mirror then a triple. The luxurious thick fringe framed their eyes and really did make them look dramatic!

Looking like movie stars, the girls then headed into the kitchen to browse for a treat to bring to the backyard flock. Nancy Jo cut thick slices off an extra juicy watermelon that was sitting out on the counter. The flock couldn't eat the ripe watermelon fast enough! Cornflake hid away an extra slice for herself for later. It was her favorite!

After a very fun-filled visit, it was time for Betsy and Lynette to leave. Nancy Jo said her goodbyes to her Aunt Elaine and Aunt Mimi, her uncles, and her cousins. "Come and visit again soon!" Nancy Jo told them as they pulled out of the driveway.

"Nancy Jo, will you help me clean up this mess?" Ranger asked.

"Okay, Dad," replied Nancy Jo. Together they tidied up the kitchen and did the dishes.

Cornflake uncovered her secret stash of watermelon hidden underneath the pine shavings. After energizing herself with the refreshing juicy watermelon, she got right back to pouring herself into her full-time job of mothering. It was important to give her young pupils a proper education. She taught them everything she could think of for survival in the backyard. At night, Cornflake called her babies with a special cluck and even though they were getting downright huge, they still wanted to cram themselves under her comforting wings at bedtime. When dusk fell, Cornflake looked drained as she kissed her babies goodnight. Then they piled in tightly under her wings for the night.

When Nancy Jo returned to the hen house the next morning, she noticed Cornflake had dark circles under her eyes and her thinning feathers looked a mess. Being a mom was hard work!

"Oh, Cornflake, I know what you need!" she said. "You need a Mommy Makeover!"

She scooped up Cornflake and rushed her inside for a well-deserved miracle beauty treatment. Nancy Jo started by washing Cornflake's dirty feet with some gentle shampoo. Then she dipped Cornflake into a luxurious bubble bath.

Cornflake had never soaked in a bubble bath before, and she wasn't sure she liked this part of the beauty treatment, but Nancy Jo was done in a jiffy. She wrapped Cornflake in a soft cotton towel like a baby burrito and squeezed her to soak up the excess bath water from her wet feathers. Next, it was time for a blowout. Nancy Jo set her hair dryer on the lowest setting and blow-dried Cornflake's feathers until they were shiny and fluffy.

Cornflake felt like a goddess and her fresh face radiated such joy! Nancy Jo set Cornflake on the vanity, so she could see her reflection in the ornate, vintage mirror above the sink. Cornflake had to admit, she looked as cute as a button. No, on second thought, she looked drop dead gorgeous! She was thrilled with her transformation from tired mom to hen hottie, and to top it all off, Nancy Jo painted Cornflake's toe nails a crisp shade of candy apple red. Cornflake, felt young, refreshed, and beautiful!

Classy Claws

Early Sunday morning, as Nancy Jo was outside at the hen house gathering up chicken eggs, she wondered what style of eggs Ranger would cook for breakfast this morning. Her stomach was making growling noises.

It was a Sunday tradition. Upon returning to the cottage from the Sunday morning service at their tiny country church, Ranger would make as he called it, his "Sunday Egg Surprise." Ranger could whip up the fluffiest omelets, and he knew how to fry perfect over easy eggs. Since there was always an abundance

61

of eggs, Ranger experimented with an assortment of delicious egg recipes and often rotated the Sunday menu with his latest egg dish. Last Sunday was his "Killer Quiche Lorraine." Ranger had several egg recipes up his sleeve. His Scotch Eggs were boiled eggs swaddled in country pork sausage then rolled into crushed cornflakes and deep-fried. They were a real treat!

Even though Nancy Jo was a whiz at baking, she was still learning how to cook. She could make a few simple dishes and made a mean mac and cheese, but that was about it. As far as making eggs she obviously needed more practice. Her scrambled eggs were not fluffy like Ranger's and resemble the loose gravel she pours around the duck pond. And she always broke the yoke when she flipped her own over easy style eggs. Not willing to eat her own unappetizing creations, she gladly left the egg cooking to Ranger who enjoyed surprising Nancy Jo with his "egg-cellent" breakfast buffets!

This morning she found Twinkie's nest of eggs in a messy pile. She couldn't bring herself to eat them for breakfast, although she had heard from someone that duck eggs were actually very tasty. Looking at the growing collection of Twinkie's eggs, she picked them up and tossed them into the nearby woods, "Now that's tidier," she muttered to herself and hurried off to get ready for church.

At church before the service started, Nancy Jo chatted with the friendly, down to earth church people and held as many babies as she possibly could. Ranger passed out a few cartons of extra chicken eggs to whoever happened to need them that week. During the church service, Nancy Jo's mind wandered a bit as she daydreamed about getting a couple more baby chicks. *Well, why not?* She thought. *I don't have a human sister but I can have lots of hen sisters!* Nancy Jo kept quiet, but she was ecstatic with the idea! She had a hard time containing her excitement and was restlessly squirming in her seat by the end of the service.

Back at Cork Pine Cottage, Nancy Jo promptly changed out of her uncomfortable church clothes and into a loose comfy t-shirt and ripped blue jeans. Then she headed to the backyard to visit her fine feathered friends. Pancake and Twinkie didn't even notice Nancy Jo as their eyes stayed glued on a lone turkey hen walking by the run. They watched her with interest until they saw Nancy Jo. Then they gaily began bobbing their heads and quacking. They knew it was snack time!

After snack time, Nancy Jo peeked in on Cornflake and the baby ducklings and let them out of their kennel to play. She could tell by the duckling's brand-new quacks, that two of the three were girls. Since they loved water so much, she decided to name the two girls Sippy and Dippy, and she named the little boy Damp.

Cornflake milled about on the thick grass with her now teenager sized babies. Sippy, Dippy, and Damp followed close behind her like always and pleading with her, "We wanna go swimming, Mom. Will you take us swimming? Pleeeeeease?"

Nancy Jo still kept Cornflake and her ducklings separate from the rest of the flock to protect the ducklings from petty squabbles and pecking order drama. The established flock could get crabby if the new ducklings suddenly joined their exclusive *backyard club.* The hens had a strict pecking order where each knew their place from the lowliest chicken to the top chicken. Nancy Jo knew the flock would not readily accept strange baby ducklings. So, to keep peace within the flock and to avoid scraps and scrapes, Sippy, Dippy, and Damp were free to roam outside as they pleased, at least while Nancy Jo was able to keep a watchful eye on them.

The rest of the flock gawked at them from inside the enclosed run. Twinkie piped up when she saw Cornflake.

"What makes *you* so special? Why do *you* get to hog whole backyard to yourself?"

Cornflake patiently overlooked Twinkie's cutting remark. She didn't take it personally and could sympathize with Twinkie's feelings. Cornflake had to admit, she did feel like Nancy Jo's favorite girl roaming free with her overgrown babies. Twinkie's remark didn't ruffle her feathers a bit. Nothing could burst through the blissful bubble she was floating in. Overflowing with the joy of a proud mother hen, she didn't even notice her flock mates shooting jealous glares at her like poisonous darts.

The flock had adjusted to living inside the enclosed run as it was spacious enough and comfortable, but the run was no match to the wild, blooming countryside! They were happy inside the run but at the same time they missed their backyard adventures and being free to roam all the nooks and crannies that the entire country estate had to offer.

It didn't help that Pancake and Twinkie could see the carefree flocks of wild mallard ducks and Canadian geese peacefully floating down the river. The chicken sisters missed scuffling in the woods and their secret ditch, and Twinkie missed her grassy spot in the meadow and longed to take a romantic stroll with Pancake by the now flowering riverbank.

"Nancy Jo!" hollered Ranger from the kitchen window. "Breakfast is ready!"

Nancy Jo eagerly ran inside; the thick, delicious aroma of bacon filled the air. The two sat down in the sunny kitchen around an old country table, and they enjoyed a feast of French toast with warm maple syrup, buttered eggs and bacon served up with generous sides of fresh fruit salad, and if that was not enough there were warm scones with homemade strawberry-rhubarb jam and zesty orange juice!

8

The Visitor

Duck Mom
67

Later that evening, Nancy Jo went to "tuck in" her flock for the night. She noticed Penelope and Cookie taking turns dust bathing inside the old tire. Penelope had mourned the painful loss of her chicken sister Jellybean for some time now and was still learning how to live without her. Penelope, still struggling with waves of deep sadness, realized her fun sister Jellybean would want her to be happy. At that moment, Penelope decided she would live out the rest of her chicken days to the fullest! Even though Penelope would always treasure her precious memories of Jellybean, she couldn't allow herself to wallow any longer in the quicksand of sorrow or let it swallow her alive.

As Penelope embraced life again, she could now clearly see the wonderful friend she had right in front of her beak. As if seeing Cookie for the first time, Penelope turned to her, "Want to share an apple with me?"

Happy to have a hen friend, Cookie bit off a crunchy mouthful. "We're best hens now!" exclaimed Penelope.

Cookie squawked back, "Best hens forever!"

The two new besties clucked harmoniously as they pecked away at the crunchy apple and polished it off down to the core. Nancy Jo was pleased to see the budding friendship between Penelope and Cookie. It was nice to hear Penelope's cheerful clucks again! As the hens played together Nancy Jo stooped down and gave each of them a squeezy "hen hug."

As dusk started to fall, Nancy Jo checked in on Cornflake, Sippy, Dippy, and Damp. She worried about them as they were separate from the others. Not being able to put them in the main run was a problem. Even if she could put them into the main run without the worry of petty poultry drama, she knew that five ducks would be a tight squeeze. She just didn't have the extra room.

Sippy, Dippy, and Damp were now approaching adulthood, and they still wanted to huddle underneath Cornflake's wings at bedtime. Half stuffed under Cornflake's protective wings, their lower bodies no longer fit and stuck out every which way. Cornflake tried her best to cover the lumpy pile of ducks, but she was only so big!

Chuckling, Nancy Jo said good night to Cornflake, Sippy, Dippy, and Damp. Then she double-checked the lock on their dog kennel, and the remaining flock moved inside the hen house for the night. Nancy Jo gave Butterscotch, Penelope and Cookie a quick pat and locked them securely inside with Twinkie and Pancake.

Nancy Jo moved inside for the night too. Inside the cottage master bedroom was a king-sized antique iron bed where Nancy Jo's mom used to sleep. Ranger, still grieving, couldn't bring himself to sleep in it and preferred to sleep in the guest bedroom. The huge bed was made up with a colorful "strawberry patch" patchwork quilt with matching pillow shams. Her mother, a talented seamstress, had hand sewn every single square while she was bedridden for several months. The quilt had happy squares of fabric printed with cheerful wild red strawberries along with contrasting squares with buttery shades of creamy yellow and red gingham. Nancy Jo liked to curl up on the cheerful quilt and watch TV. Somehow it made her feel closer to her mother.

Off the master bedroom was a sliding screened door wall open to the backyard air. As dusk fell and the darkness of night crept in, the backyard became alive, humming with nighttime sounds of chirping crickets, croaking bullfrogs and honking wild geese echoing off the river like a country symphony. Nancy Jo popped an industrial sized bowl of hot, buttery popcorn and then flopped down on the soft oversized bed to watch one of her favorite TV shows. Nancy Jo's cheeks were so stuffed with crunchy popcorn she could barely hear the TV.

In between noisy mouthfuls of salty popcorn, Nancy Jo thought she heard something unusual coming from the backyard. Then a shrill scream, like that of a woman screaming out in pain, abruptly startled her. The eerie, high-pitched scream was unmistakable, Vixen was back!

Nancy Jo jumped up and ran to the screen door. She opened the door a crack. Just outside the door there was an old stone wall and on the top ledge of the wall sat that sneaky fox! Nancy Jo was now eyeball to eyeball with Vixen.

Vixen fixed her stare on Nancy Jo. She didn't run away, she just stood there right by the door studying Nancy Jo. Nancy Jo was not only shaken by the unexpected wild screams, but she was also surprised by the extreme intelligence she saw in Vixen's eyes and her curiosity about humans. Vixen's probing eyes felt like they were looking right through her. Suddenly Vixen let out another forceful high-pitched scream. A strange eerie feeling came over Nancy Jo, as she got a whiff of Vixen's rank perfume. She had never been so close to a shrieking wild animal before even though she was still standing in her mom's bedroom!

Nancy Jo noticed something move a few feet away in the dark. As she turned on the outside light, she discovered it was her cat, Clyde. Vixen screamed more vehemently. Clyde stood still, frozen in fear. He didn't budge. Vixen seemed to be screaming at Clyde for some reason, but why?

Nancy Jo, now worried about Clyde and unsure what to do,

called out to her dad, "Come quick!"

Ranger rushed in, and they peeked out again. This time they saw Vixen near the woods, hunched over. Her front paws were clutching something—it was a duck egg! Vixen was eating the duck eggs Nancy Jo had thrown in the woods. Now Nancy Jo understood why Vixen was letting off a musky scent. She was marking her territory and protecting her bountiful treasure trove of eggs. She ravenously crammed down her prize, a paw-licking egg supper! Nancy Jo and her dad watched Vixen hungrily devour every single egg.

Inside the dog kennel, Cornflake, Sippy, Dippy, and Damp heard Vixen's screams. They snuggled together even tighter and were glad to be safely locked up tight in the dog kennel. The rest of the flock was nervous too knowing Vixen was stalking nearby, and nearby by she was!

Vixen quietly slunk right up to the hen house. She pressed her face against the protective thick metal screen, her green eyes flickering in the dark. With a mocking tone in her voice, she whispered, "Thank you for the duck eggs, Twinkie, but now I am craving Duck a L'Orange!"

Twinkie's knees began to knock together as Vixen's blood-thirsty words sent an icy chill through her body. She could feel goosebumps forming on her tender skin clear through her thick down feathers.

Pancake had heard enough out of Vixen, and he rushed to Twinkie's side. "Don't be afraid, Twinkie. Vixen can't touch you in here. Don't let her scare you!"

With a cold hard stare, Vixen cruelly threatened Twinkie. "I always get what I want, and I'm coming back for you." Vixen then turned on her heel and silently disappeared into the darkness.

Butterscotch, Penelope, and Cookie now roused from their sleep came down from their roost to the ground floor to comfort Twinkie who was now in tears. "You are perfectly safe, Twinkie," reassured Butterscotch. "I guess that's why Nancy Jo and Ranger don't let us free-range anymore."

The flock became instantly more grateful for their enclosure and now understood that Nancy Jo and Ranger didn't actually want to take away their fun or freedom. Nancy Jo and Ranger just wanted to protect them. Twinkie had a change of attitude after that night.

The next morning two curious Canadian geese came up to the run. "Greetings!" "What are you doing in there?" asked one of the geese.

Twinkie explained. "Pekin ducks and chickens can't fly like geese can. I'm in here because Nancy Jo loves me and wants me to be safe."

"Oh, very splendid indeed," nodded the geese agreeably, as they flapped their wings and took flight. As they flew off, they hollered down to Twinkie, "Fare thee well, lucky duck!"

Twinkie looked up at them and quacked back, "I *am* a lucky duck!"

Proud Mom

The next morning, Nancy Jo and Ranger headed out to the local farm supply store. Nancy Jo's 4-H Club friends were at the store holding a fundraiser to help support the local animal shelters in the area. The 4-H club donated whatever they could—handmade crafts, baked goods, seed packets, potted plants and flowers—to sell to raise money. Nancy Jo brought several dozen cupcakes that she had baked herself to donate to the fundraiser and of course, fresh eggs.

Once inside, Nancy Jo noticed there were huge stock tanks in the center of the store filled with different varieties of baby chicks and ducklings. It was a stroke of luck! The store was holding its seasonal "Chick Days" event. Ranger knew Nancy Jo couldn't resist and went off to shop for wild bird seed, "woodpecker blend" suet cakes, and dog food for their small mob of dogs, Biscuit a fourteen-year-old yellow lab, Eddie a younger tank sized yellow lab, and Tucker a rescued Australian Shepherd.

Nancy Jo set her cupcakes and eggs down on top of the fundraiser table and excused herself. "I'll be right back."

With baby chicks on the brain, she became lost in her thoughts. She knew she couldn't take in anymore ducks, but surely a couple more baby chicks wouldn't hurt. She also knew she would have to do something about Sippy, Dippy, and Damp because she had more than she could handle with just the two ducks, Twinkie and Pancake. The ducks required a lot of extra work since they were not only messy but needed an abundance of water in order to swallow their food and to dunk their heads, not to mention swimming and splashing. She loved Twinkie and Pancake, but she felt overwhelmed with the responsibility of meeting their great need for water. She didn't think she could keep up with three more, particularly in the wintertime when it was much harder to care for the flock.

The chickens were much lower maintenance. They were much tidier and didn't need the endless twenty-four-hour water buffets like the ducks. Nancy Jo pondered about her duck problem as she walked with long strides back to the stock tanks. As she gazed inside the stock tanks filled with innocent little fuzz balls, something in her animal loving heart began to stir. Overcome with wonder and admiration, Nancy Jo forgot all about the fundraiser. Caught up in the moment, she couldn't help herself. She thought, *I have to get a couple more. Just a couple more.*

Nancy Jo looked serious as she compared the different breeds of chicks available. It was tough picking out baby chicks. She only had room in her hen house for two more chickens, and knowing she could only get two seemed impossible. She stood by the stock tanks and watched them for a while.

"Can I help you?" asked the store attendant.

"I'm still trying to make up my mind," answered Nancy Jo.

Nancy Jo read the signs detailing the different breeds. She even did a quick search on her phone about the Easter Egger chicks offered for sale. She found out they can lay blue eggs. Well, that did it for her. She wanted one of those. She did another search on her phone for the breed Barred Plymouth Rocks. Nancy Jo learned they have a calm temperament and that they lay large eggs. Well, that sounded good to her. She also read that they are an old breed dating back to 1849. "Oh!" she thought. "I must have one of those too!"

She picked out her two favorites and called the attendant back over to assist her. The attendant placed the innocent chicks into a cardboard carrier for Nancy Jo. The alert baby hatchlings intently peeked out through the carrier's air holes trying to get a good look at Nancy Jo.

Excited with her livestock purchase, she headed to the fundraiser table with her new pets. Running a bit behind schedule, she was already supposed to be there helping out.

"Distracted much?" one of her 4-H friends teased. "It's okay we pretty much have it covered anyhow."

"I'm sorry, you guys!" said Nancy Jo as she sat down at the fundraiser table. "I'll get to work." Nancy Jo waited on one customer and then was busy showing off her hatchlings to her 4-H friends when her neighbor Kenny came up to the table.

Nancy Jo had a secret crush on Kenny. The problem was so did most of the other girls at school. Kenny was in the ninth grade and had expressive soft brown eyes and dark thick wavy hair. His handsome "Prince Charming" features were finely chiseled like an artist's sculpture. Kenny and another girl from school had ridden their bikes into town.

"I'll take a few of those cupcakes," said Kenny with a sincere smile. "A banana nut, a chocolate, and I think I'll try a strawberry rhubarb."

Kenny was always kind, and the girl he was with was nothing short of stunning with a dark tan, flashy white teeth, and long silky light blonde hair. Nancy Jo had seen her around at school, but she didn't know her name. She thought "Malibu Barbie" would be fitting.

"Thank you for supporting the animal shelters, Kenny," said Nancy Jo as she handed him the cupcakes in a small bakery box.

Kenny pointed to the cardboard carrier with air holes. "What do you have in there?" he asked.

"A couple baby chicks," said Nancy Jo as she opened up the box for Kenny to get a peek.

"Wow, they are so cool! I wish I could have chickens. My dad said no more pets, but I think I can change his mind."

"Tell him you won't have to buy eggs at the grocery store anymore," said Nancy Jo. "That could help."

Kenny and the girl left and another girl from 4-H Club came in and relieved Nancy Jo of her duties at the fundraising table. Nancy Jo went to search for Ranger and found him in the dog food aisle lifting a fifty-pound bag of dog food into the cart.

"Oh, there you are!" she said. "I have new babies!" She opened the cardboard carrier and showed off her newly hatched chicks.

Ranger didn't seem surprised at all and admired the cute little chickies alongside Nancy Jo. "Whatever makes you happy, Darlin'," he said in a matter-of-fact voice. He knew Nancy Jo's love for animals.

"Look what I found for your flock," said Ranger as he pulled an item out of the shopping cart. "The clerk told me these just hit the shelves!"

"Wow! That is so cool!" shrieked Nancy Jo as she laid eyes on the bright pink chicken harness and matching leash. It was just what her flock needed. Now she could take her chickens and even her ducks on walking adventures!

On the way home Nancy Jo chose names for her new chicks. Since there was an abundance of rhubarb growing around the cottage, she named the baby Barred Rock chick, Rhubarb. As she studied the Easter Egger chick, she took note of her plump body which was full and rounded, so she thought Dumplin would be a suitable name for her.

Back at the cottage Nancy Jo got Rhubarb and Dumplin settled into their temporary brooder box home in the cottage bathroom, complete with fresh pine shavings and a small feeder and waterer. As she dashed off to look for the brooder heat lamp, Rhubarb and Dumplin stretched out and relaxed a bit. They sensed they were in good hands with Nancy Jo. When Nancy Jo returned with the brooder lamp, she found the two baby chicks nestled together and fast asleep.

9

Duckling Debut

Cornflake And Company

In the backyard, Sippy, Dippy, and Damp joyfully waddled behind Cornflake single file around the yard. Now almost young adults, the devoted trio of ducks still clung close to their beloved mom. Nancy Jo looked on with a sad pang in her heart, knowing it was time for Sippy, Dippy, and Damp to leave Cork Pine Cottage. She didn't have room in her modest run for five ducks along with the chickens. Also, she didn't think she could endure the added work of taking care of them.

Bill Green, a friend of Ranger's, offered to take Sippy, Dippy, and Damp to live at his farm, Green Pastures. Plenty of other ducks as well as horses and a variety of small farm animals lived at his farm. With expansive acreage, the farm could easily afford to adopt a few more ducks and most importantly, Nancy Jo knew they would be well cared for. It was a hard decision to make, but Nancy Jo knew it was the best decision for the well-being of the ducklings. Fighting back tears, she dreaded telling Cornflake the news. She only hoped the hen would understand.

Green Pastures also served the community as a therapy camp for troubled kids from age eight to eighteen. Nancy Jo herself, filled with overwhelming pain after losing her mom, had stayed at the camp. The loving counselors had rallied around her and still checked in on her from time to time. Green Pastures offered a safe place for kids to visit and to get the extra help they needed to grow up happy and well-adjusted. The supportive camp counselors treated the visitors like family and the troubled kids no longer had to carry the heavy weight of their problems all alone. The kids who visited the camp came from all different backgrounds. Some were from broken homes. Some were orphans from foster homes. And some, like Nancy Jo just needed some extra tender loving care.

At the farm, a counselor was assigned to help each kid, one on one, to help them overcome the difficult challenges they faced. The counselors were caring, well-trained professionals and the personal secrets of the visitors were held in the strictest confidence. The kids, like tender plants, came to the farm in a fragile state but received the water of life they needed to thrive.

Green Pastures gained the respect of the surrounding communities as a positive influence for kids. People took notice of so many restored young lives. The generous land not only had farm animals but its own chapel and a small onsite store that sold bait and convenience items right on the property. The kids enjoyed camping in tents, fishing in the creek, roasting marshmallows over a campfire, and even horseback riding.

After deciding Green Pastures would be the best home for Sippy, Dippy, and Damp, Nancy Jo spent some precious time with them. She tossed them some Cheerios and watched them play a game of Hide-and-Seek for a while before she went back inside the cottage.

Following Mom

Later that night, with Cornflake and the ducklings on her mind, Nancy Jo became troubled and couldn't sleep. She couldn't take Sippy, Dippy, and Damp away from their mom, but she also felt like she didn't have a choice. She tossed and turned and then rolled over for the last time and fell into a deep sleep.

She dreamt about taking Cornflake, Sippy, Dippy, and Damp to visit the senior center. In her dream, she lugged the heavy travel crate of feathered critters into the senior center and plunked it down on the hard floor. Cornflake hopped out first, followed by Sippy, Dippy, and Damp. Nancy Jo picked them up and sat them atop a long table so everyone could see them. Then she placed a microphone on a tall stand in front of them.

In the dream, Nancy Jo opened a fancy gift-wrapped box and surprised them with tiny Bavarian outfits custom-made for each of them. She dressed Cornflake, Sippy, and Dippy in traditional Bavarian style ruffled apron dresses, also known as dirndls. First, she slipped over their heads a frilly white bodice style blouse with puffy sleeves. Then she donned them each with a pair of bloomers and a poofy petticoat underskirt. After dressing them in the fancy undergarments, she layered colorful sleeveless pinafores over top the crisp frilly blouses. The dirndl pinafores were checkered with bright blue and white checks and laced up the front like a corset. Then Nancy Jo tied tiny frilly white aprons on them to complete the look. Damp wore traditional lederhosen, leather shorts with suspenders over a crisp white shirt and boxer briefs. The lederhosen were colorfully decorated with exquisite embroidery, and he looked so handsome!

Cornflake whispered something into Nancy Jo's ear. Nancy Jo nodded and then turned to the crowd and cordially announced, "Introducing Cornflake and The Quackers! "Let's give them a big round of applause!"

The lunch bunch cheered and clapped with much enthusiasm, admiring the animals adorned in festive German style fashion. The ducklings were nothing short of stunning, and they beamed with pride. Cornflake dazzled like a true Bavarian belle as she moved to the edge of the table and took center stage. With a boost of confidence from the crowd, Cornflake signaled her babies with a nod and Sippy, Dippy, and Damp began to quack in a rhythmic harmony. Then Cornflake belted out her own made-up song.

"My name is Cornflake and
I'm here for Show and Tell
And all I have to say is
I've been blessed very well
I wanted to be a mom, you see
And bounce fuzzy baby
chicks on my knee
For many long weeks on
my nest did I camp
Until I hatched Sippy, Dippy, and Damp
My chickens quack, but I don't care
And now they're wearing underwear!"

The lunch bunch crowd clapped wildly! Cornflake, Sippy, Dippy, and Damp enjoyed their moment in the spotlight. Nancy Jo was surprised by her flock's talent. *How could I not have known my flock was so talented?* she thought. She was most impressed with Cornflake's stellar performance! Cornflake took a bow and nudged Sippy, Dippy, and Damp to do the same. They all took a low bow as they soaked up the appreciative applause.

Nancy Jo's cat, Clyde, impatiently pawed at Nancy Jo's cheek until she began to stir. It was time for his morning cat food snack, which was half a can of wet cat food. Clyde persisted until Nancy Jo's eyes started to open.

Groggy, Nancy Jo remembered her dream. "What on earth did I eat last night?" she wondered. But she also realized her dream, part crazy, had a bit of truth. She loved her flock so much, and she wanted everyone else to love her ordinary flock as much as she did. They were superstars in her eyes. The dream inspired in her to give Cornflake and her brood a day of honor. She would take them with her for Show and Tell at the senior center!

Nancy Jo gave Clyde and her other cat, Gemma, their cat food snacks and poured herself a tall, eye-opening glass of orange juice. Looking forward to bringing Cornflake, Sippy, and Damp to Show and Tell, she showered and got ready for her volunteer job in the bathroom she shared with Rhubarb and Dumplin. Then she headed to the backyard to tell Cornflake her plan.

"Cornflake, I want to take you to work with me today at the senior center!"

Surprised, Cornflake clucked with glee! "Can Sippy, Dippy, and Damp come too?" she asked.

"Of course, they can," said Nancy Jo.

So, it was settled. Cornflake and her beloved ducklings would have their own day of honor at the senior center for Show and Tell! Giddy with anticipation, Nancy Jo hurriedly emptied and refilled the stock tank duck pond and gave the flock their morning snacks.

Nancy Jo loaded the bulky travel crate into the back of Ranger's truck. Then, one at a time, she carried Sippy, Dippy, and Damp and placed them inside. Nancy Jo placed Cornflake in the front passenger seat and then squeezed herself into the middle between Ranger and Cornflake.

Nancy Jo turned to Cornflake. "We can't leave until I buckle you in." Then she strapped the seat belt around Cornflake's chest. The seat belt squarely held Cornflake in the seat. She was too short to see out the window, but she felt very important riding shotgun in the front with Nancy Jo!

The truck radio played a catchy tune and added to Cornflake's bright cheerful mood, but her mood was rudely interrupted by a disturbing commercial. "Bring the whole family in for the *all you can eat* fried chicken dinner special at The Chicken Leg Cafeteria!" The announcer's words felt like a stinging slap in the beak! Cornflake's heart sank! It wasn't fair! Chickens should NEVER BE FRIED!

Stunned, Cornflake's head drooped as a wave of sadness came over her and the pit of her stomach twisted into a knot. Her usual sweet face curdled into a sour pout as she numbly stared at the floor.

"We're here!" said Nancy Jo to Cornflake as they pulled into the parking lot. Nancy Jo unbuckled Cornflake and cradled her in her arms.

Cornflake lifted her head and became filled with curiosity as she laid eyes on the mysterious senior center. Excited all over again, she put her hurt chicken feelings aside. She couldn't wait to see the inside and debut her darling ducklings.

At the senior center, Nancy Jo plunked down the heavy crate and got right to work. She was busy wiping down the tables when her good friend Mary Kay came in to help. It could get quite busy, and Nancy Jo was grateful her classmate and friend since kindergarten showed up to volunteer with her.

"Hi, Mary Kay! I'm so glad you're here."

"Me too!" said Mary Kay. "It looks like you're swamped!" Mary Kay was always eager to lend a hand, and she was so patient and helpful with the senior citizens.

Nancy Jo and Mary Kay buzzed around like busy bees. They helped load the volunteer delivery drivers with Meals on Wheels for the local elderly shut-ins. Then it was time to set the long tables. The girls piled generous portions of fresh baked goods on trays and got the coffee ready.

Just as the coffee began to trickle down from the coffee maker, the seniors began to trickle in too. The luncheon was served at 11:30 a.m. sharp, and Cornflake, Sippy, Dippy, and Damp stayed inside the travel crate while the people sat down to dine. Nancy Jo and Mary Kay served up piping hot bowls of chili to the "lunch bunch" as they liked to call them.

"It looks like a good meal today," Joyce commented as Nancy Jo set down a sectioned plate in front of her filled with a green salad, a buttermilk biscuit, a fresh apple, and a dainty dessert. Dessert was not often served as part of the luncheon, but today everyone enjoyed a rich molded, molten chocolate lava cake. It was warm, with a gooey, fudgey center!

Watching the whirlwind of activity from inside the crate, Cornflake let out a thankful sigh of relief as she observed the seniors eating lunch. She was glad they weren't eating some kind of chicken. She didn't think her stomach could take another scandal. "A chicken's life matters too!" she told herself. Sensitive in nature, Cornflake felt the wrongs of chicken injustice deeply and took it personally. She would never want herself or her chicken sisters to be fried into tenders or even worse, put into a casserole!

After the nutritious meal, the close-knit lunch bunch sipped coffee, nibbled fresh baked goods, and shared a lot of laughs together. Nancy Jo suspected they enjoyed their social time even more than the food itself. Many of the seniors had become widows or widowers, and they cherished their deep friendships and enjoyed sharing the ups and downs of life together.

The lighthearted chatter quieted down for a grown-up version of Show and Tell. Nancy Jo and Mary Kay cleared off the long tables and sat with the others. First up was Ben. He brought in his army uniform from 1949. He was full of World War II stories and interesting history. Next, Irma brought in her beautiful framed wedding photo from seventy-five years ago. Her husband had passed many years ago, but she treasured her memories of him. Nancy Jo was shocked to see Irma's face in the photo, so young and radiant looking. She was a breathtaking bride!

After Irma finished sharing her wedding photo, Nancy Jo unlocked Cornflake's travel crate. Out popped Cornflake, Sippy, Dippy, and Damp! All eyes were glued on them which made Cornflake feel a wee bit shy at first. But the warm, welcoming people set her at ease.

They oohed and aah-ed and gushed over all of them. They wanted to hold them and spoil them with whatever treats they could find—scraps of leftover lettuce, apple slices, and bits of buttermilk biscuits. The lunch bunch marveled at the unusual family and how the ducklings formed a perfect line following Cornflake wherever she went. Nancy Jo was proud of her flock. Like in her dream, they were well-behaved, and she was pleased the lunch bunch showered her ordinary flock with such love!

Old man Fred was the last to share for Show and Tell. It was obvious what he brought, with an accordion tucked under his arm. Old man Fred always wowed the crowd with his skillful playing on the accordion. He said he had learned to play by watching an old variety show on TV called The Lawrence Welk Show. He still enjoyed watching the old reruns from a bygone era, and he played everything by ear!

Fred announced he had a certain song in mind to play in honor of their feathered guests. So, without further ado, Fred exuberantly began to play a popular party song, none other than The Chicken Dance Polka! Once that jubilant tune started to ring out, the lunch crowd couldn't resist joining in. Even Nancy Jo and Mary Kay got in on the fun! They formed a circle and channeled their best inner chicken. The delighted senior citizens danced like teenagers. They clucked, flapped their wings, and shook their tail feathers! During the slow part of the song, they partnered off with the person standing next to them, locked elbows, and spun in joyful circles. It was the best day of Show and Tell Nancy Jo could remember!

10

Green Pastures

Dumplin

Rhubarb and Dumpling were busy growing up in the bathroom. Rhubarb was very social. She enjoyed hitchhiking on Nancy Jo's shoulder around the house and running her beak through Nancy Jo's hair. Rhubarb was curious about Nancy Jo's other pet birds, Popcorn the cockatiel and Pee Wee the parakeet.

Nancy Jo decided to introduce them one day while the small pet birds were getting some loose "fly time" in the sitting room. Rhubarb slowly approached Popcorn. Her eyes were quickly drawn to the vibrant orange patches on Popcorn's cheeks and her tiny bright blue sidekick, Pee Wee.

As Rhubarb edged closer, Popcorn felt threatened as Rhubarb looked like a giant T-Rex! In an attempt to appear massive and menacing, Popcorn instinctively spread his wings out as far as they would stretch. Popcorn appeared pitifully small next to Rhubarb, and he felt afraid. As Popcorn looked Rhubarb square in the eyes, he noticed Rhubarb's sweet gentleness. Even though she was a giant in comparison, she had come in peace.

Popcorn's jittery fears quietly faded into curiosity. The two locked eyes and engaged in a polite but intense staring contest. They became stiff like frozen bird statues as they stared at one another in amazement. Peewee, who didn't like the looks of Rhubarb, flew away and perched on top of her birdcage to watch from a safe distance.

Dumplin, Nancy Jo's lap chicken, liked to cuddle. She preferred cuddling on Nancy Jo's lap in front of the TV above all else. She especially enjoyed Judge Judy. The two hens were content being pampered indoors. Still a bit small to go outside, Nancy Jo wanted to savor her time with her indoor chicks since it wouldn't be long before they would be fully feathered and ready for the backyard.

She enjoyed seeing them in the bathroom every day. She

could pop in for a visit anytime, and as she showered, Rhubarb would wait for her perched on the edge of the tub. The curious hens sat on top of the bathroom sink vanity and watched Nancy Jo fix her hair and get ready for the day. They wondered what she was putting on her face.

"What is that stuff?" asked Rhubarb.

"It's called makeup," said Nancy Jo as she added a touch of creamy lipstick. "It's supposed to help me look beautiful."

Rhubarb and Dumplin didn't understand why Nancy Jo needed to wear makeup. Neither did Ranger for that matter, but Nancy Jo liked to experiment with different makeup looks. Rhubarb and Dumplin liked Nancy Jo just fine without any stuff on her face. Nancy Jo gave them each a little kiss, leaving a red lipstick print of her lips on each of their heads and headed to the kitchen.

Rhubarb

Ranger was talking on the phone with someone. "Okay, I will bring them with me today and drop them off on the way to work," he said before he hung up. Ranger poured Nancy Jo a healthy smoothie he whipped up in the blender made with Greek yogurt, frozen strawberries, and bananas to which Nancy Jo added two generous long squirts of chocolate syrup.

"You remember Bill Green from Green Pastures Farm?" said

93

Ranger. "Well, that was him. He asked if I could drop off the ducks on my way in to work."

Nancy Jo could hardly believe the day had come when Sippy, Dippy, and Damp would move away. She chugged down her smoothie as fast as she could; she needed to get to the backyard! The throbbing pain of brain freeze gripped her skull, but Nancy Jo didn't have time to waste. Not bothering to grab her coat, she ran outside.

Nancy Jo let Cornflake, Sippy, Dippy, and Damp free-range in the backyard together one last time. Nancy Jo took a few pictures and watched the contented little family. With happy clucks and quacks, they slowly meandered around the lawn now strewn with colored leaves. Fall was here and it was time to say goodbye.

With a heavy heart Nancy Jo rounded up Cornflake, Sippy, Dippy, and Damp and placed them in the travel crate. Cornflake had a bewildered look on her face as Damp plunged into the crock pot of water placed inside the crate. *Why do my chicks love to swim so much?* she wondered.

Nancy Jo interrupted her thoughts. "Cornflake, I have some bad news."

Cornflake peered through the grate of the travel crate at Nancy Jo.

"I'm sorry to tell you this, but winter will be here soon, and we aren't set up to keep your babies here at Cork Pine Cottage. Ranger will be taking them to a top-notch farm that helps troubled kids."

Cornflake felt the weight of Nancy Jo's words. This was the end of her motherhood! Stunned at the news, her little knees went weak. A woozy feeling came over her as her fragile heart shattered into pieces, three duck shaped pieces to be exact. This couldn't be happening! Cornflake, frozen in shock, helplessly watched Nancy Jo load her babies into the travel crate inside the back of Ranger's pick up. Her sad eyes blurred with tears.

Then Nancy Jo surprised Cornflake as she scooped her up too and placed her inside the crate with Sippy, Dippy, and Damp. A temporary wave of relief washed over Cornflake as she scrambled to nestle close to her teenage babies. Sippy, Dippy, and Damp snuggled tight against their mom's soft familiar feathers as Cornflake showered them with sweet kisses. Suddenly, the truck began to move.

Ranger headed towards the farm with a twinge of sadness in his heart. He would miss those cute little quackers, but he knew Green Pastures was a more suitable home for Sippy, Dippy, and Damp. It had plenty of room for them to roam free since there was electric fencing surrounding and protecting an area of several acres, and they would enjoy seeing all the kids that visited.

Ranger's truck bumped along the dirt road as Cornflake and her oversized babies clung to each other. They feared the unknown and what was to become of them and their little family.

"We don't want to leave you Mom!" Sippy whimpered.

"You will all be okay," reassured Cornflake. "Nancy Jo will see to it, don't you worry!" Cornflake lovingly sang to them a comforting melody. "No matter how old you are, you'll always be my babies. No matter how far you roam, forever you will be, here in my heart. Always a part . . . of me."

Sippy, Dippy, and Damp basked in the sweet sound of Cornflake's gentle voice. Their mom's song warmed the ducklings' hearts, and they felt a cozy glow from within. Even though nothing had changed, and they were still going to live at Green Pastures, they relaxed as they felt their mom's tender love envelop them. A sweet sense of calm filled them and chased away their fears. They knew they would always be her babies, no matter what, and it gave them comfort and a burst of confidence.

Ranger made his way down the dusty dirt road and then turned into a long, winding driveway. A large sign read, "Welcome to Green Pastures." At the end of the driveway stood a very old white farmhouse with a wide inviting front porch with an old-fashioned screen door and red rocking chairs where a fat orange cat was napping. Tall stalks of dried corn husks flanked the pillars of the wooden porch steps which were dotted with cheerful pumpkins.

Just past the farm house was a little red milk house with an attached farm stand full of hand-picked corn, squash, bell peppers, and seasonal vegetables as well as a variety homemade pies, jellies, and jams. The milk house served as a small convenience store and sold night crawlers, cold pop, snacks, and bug spray.

In the background stood three picturesque red barns with crisp white trim and a tiny, white clapboard chapel with a bell tower adorned with a simple round stained-glass window.

"We're here," said Ranger. He unlocked the travel crate and picked up Cornflake and the ducklings one by one and plopped them down on the ground. Just as Sippy, Dippy, and Damp set foot on the gravel driveway, out of nowhere a whole flock of ducks joyfully waddled up to them, excited to see the farm's newest ducks. Happy quacks greeted the newcomers and made them feel welcome.

Cornflake sensed her babies would make fast friends on the farm and that they would have many good times together. She was happy for them, but a wave of sadness overcame her at the thought of going home to Cork Pine Cottage without them. She needed a good cry.

Cornflake kept a stiff upper beak as the farm ducks swarmed her beloved babies. While the ducks were all getting acquainted, she slipped behind the milk house and sobbed so hard. Her tender heart felt such searing pain, even her chicken gizzards hurt! Caught up in the excitement of the moment, the ducklings didn't notice their mom's absence. Sippy and Dippy drank in the view of the vast farm land. There were no hills like at Cork Pine Cottage but it was definitely a duck's paradise!

One of the farm ducks informed them, "We only get locked up at night in a night pen. We get to run free all day." Sippy and Dippy, overcome with delight, erupted with gleeful quacks. It was major head bobbing worthy news! As if they were being tickled, they gleefully pumped their heads up and down and enjoyed a hearty quack fest.

Damp's eyes bugged out when he noticed all the pretty girl ducks. Like the flick of a light switch, his male instincts clicked on. He noticed all the lovely ducks, but it was obvious he was already drawn to one in particular. There in front of him stood a very attractive duck with beautiful golden plumage. She was so graceful! Without thinking or caring how silly he looked, Damp strutted in front of her and tried to show off his best side. He hoped she would notice his fancy tail feathers, but the beautiful golden duck seemed unimpressed with his proud display.

Damp, certain there were definite sparks between him and the golden duck, wouldn't give up and continued to show off for her. Swaggering like a cool duck rapper, Damp did some fancy footwork and showed off his best b boy moves and rhymed to her. "I don't mean to brag, but you *know* I got swag!"

The golden duck just yawned. The more the beautiful golden duck ignored Damp's advances the more determined he was to win her over. As a last resort Damp stuck out his chest and flexed his rather skinny muscles. *Surely my superbly formed masculine physique will win her over*, he thought. But the golden duck remained aloof and unresponsive to all of Damp's efforts to woo her.

To the farm ducks Damp looked ridiculous, and they bobbed their heads and quacked with great amusement. The happy noise of the quacking ducks got Bill's attention as he was hard at work mucking out horse stalls. He emerged from one of the barns wearing dirty coveralls and a friendly toothy grin.

"Hi, Ranger," he said. "I see you already met the ducks. Let me show you around."

Bill showed Ranger the horse barn first. "Here, hop up on Old Gingerbread," said Bill.

With no previous riding experience, Ranger was a bit hesitant, but Bill insisted she was very gentle.

Ranger took a closer look at Old Gingerbread. Her color was like gingerbread all right, but her head had a splotch of white and her legs looked like they were dipped in white paint. She didn't look threatening. Her head was slightly drooped, and she let out a soft snort of contentment. "Oh, why not?" said Ranger as he jumped up into Gingerbread's saddle. Bill quickly saddled his favorite horse and off they went to explore the beautiful farm and outbuildings.

As they rode past, a young girl who was working the farm stand threw the farm ducks some loose cabbage leaves. The ducks attacked the vegetables hungrily. It was every duck for himself! Sippy, Dippy, and Damp were not quite fast enough though and missed out on the treats. They were not used to being a part of such a large flock. They would need to be faster! Luckily the alert girl noticed Sippy, Dippy, and Damp's awkward slowness.

"You must be the new ducks," she said, as she kindly hand fed them some fresh green leaves "I promise, you'll get the hang of it!"

11

Cornflake's Homecoming

Travel Crate Lodging
101

Sippy, Dippy, Damp and all the farm ducks got along splendidly. Just as they finished up a game of Duck Duck Goose, Ranger returned from his tour of the farm and Cornflake finally reappeared out of her hiding spot behind the milk house. It was time to say goodbye.

Cornflake bravely hugged Sippy, Dippy, and Damp goodbye. "I have to be strong," she told herself. She wouldn't allow herself to melt into a fit of tears and be one of those embarrassing moms in front of all the other farm ducks. "I will miss you," she said, "and I will visit you, I promise!"

Ranger knew this family parting was very hard for Cornflake. He scooped her up, gave her a little hug, and set her on the dashboard of his truck.

As Ranger pulled out the driveway, Sippy, Dippy, and Damp each flapped a single wing and slowly waved goodbye. They cried out, "We love you, Mom!"

Ranger turned to Cornflake and said, "You wanna go to work with me?" Cornflake nodded silently. Already running late for his job at the state park, Ranger hit the gas. It was his responsibility to give a lecture to the park's visitors in a half an hour.

Ranger made it to the park with five minutes to spare. He held Cornflake in his arms as he gave an educational presentation about black bears and bear safety to the visitors. Cornflake loved the individual attention she received from Ranger and the swooning visitors that day. On the way home Ranger stopped off at a nearby yogurt stand and bought Cornflake her very own cup of blackberry frozen yogurt! As she dug in, the purple yogurt dripped off her beak and splashed down her chest. Ranger blotted Cornflake with a few paper napkins and then made her a bib by tying an old blue bandanna around her neck. She enjoyed every last creamy bite.

It was mid-afternoon when Cornflake arrived back at Cork Pine Cottage. Things already seemed different to her. She felt empty, like a piece of her heart had been torn out and now all that was left was a gaping hole. Cornflake followed Ranger inside the cottage. Nancy Jo was waiting for her to return. "Oh Cornflake! I have a surprise for you! Come and see!"

With a bouncy spring in her step and a secretive smile, Nancy Jo led Cornflake out to the backyard. Cornflake gasped when she saw the hen house. Nancy Jo had totally redecorated! The plain hen house was now an enchanting cozy cottage. Cornflake couldn't believe her eyes! Nancy Jo had put a fresh lick of paint on the entire hen house while she was away.

"I hope you like it," said Nancy Jo. "I found the paint in the garage. It's called Meadow Green."

Cornflake was very pleased indeed and so was the rest of the flock. The hens even reviewed the new improved hen house among themselves like it was a fancy hotel. They gave it five out of five clucks!

"We give it a five-cluck rating!" the feathered "customers" informed Nancy Jo. Nancy Jo was pleased her "customers" were satisfied and her hard work had paid off. Nancy Jo had also found four old shutters and a couple flower boxes in the shed and painted them with a pastel shade called "English Rose," a soft petal pink.

Kenny, her hunky neighbor, had helped her hang the shutters on two of the windows and mounted the flower boxes underneath the sills. Kenny was very good at building things; he even knew how to build his own go karts. Unfortunately, Kenny never noticed how Nancy Jo's eyes lit up every time she saw him. He treated Nancy Jo like a kid sister. Kenny was so helpful that day, and he looked as handsome as ever. But he wasn't hung up on his good looks, which actually made him more attractive somehow. He had a practical mind and simply liked to be helpful.

Nancy Jo had filled the flower boxes with dirt and planted colorful dark purple mums in them. The hen house had a fresh look on the inside too. Nancy Jo used a hot glue gun to hang some vintage floral curtains and then tied them back with pink ribbons tied into bows. The cotton curtains were crisp white and delicately printed with romantic pink blooming roses with green leafy stems.

Since Cornflake would be rejoining the flock, Nancy Jo wanted her to have a welcoming homecoming. For the final touch, Nancy Jo and Kenny had hung a chicken swing from the ceiling, just for fun. The swing toy was hand made by a bighearted fellow from the little country church who had a knack for making unique wood crafts with precision.

Butterscotch and the rest of the flock were happy to have Cornflake back as one of the regular flock. They had missed her! Cornflake had to get used to being a regular flock member again. She had gotten used to having her separate living quarters, and her heart was still aching, but at the same time, she was also glad to be back home with her beloved chicken sisters, and of course, Twinkie and Pancake.

After Sunday church service Ranger pulled a hefty ten-pound baggie of ground sirloin from the fridge and began to pull hunks of meat off the huge mound and form hamburger patties for the grill. Today was the church picnic and it was being held at Cork Pine Cottage.

The church people began to pour in with coolers, kayaks,

and even the church's corn hole game. Of course, they brought lots of homemade dishes too. Nancy Jo's mouth watered when she saw the huge spread of desserts! The church folk grabbed whatever lawn furniture they could find or parked themselves on a chair under a shady umbrella table on the deck which overlooked the river below.

Ranger grilled hamburgers and hot dogs outside, and the hungry congregation quickly wolfed them all down before Ranger even brought out the condiments. Ranger had forgotten to bring out the fresh lettuce and the slices of tomato and onion he had cut up beforehand. It was all still sitting in the fridge! The ravenous church people didn't seem to notice the missing condiments, or maybe they were just too polite to mention it, but they pretty much devoured everything. The church people had hearty appetites for food and fun.

After the barbecue, the pastor invited those who wanted to be baptized down to the river. Since the cottage sat atop a steep hill, almost everyone took the walking path and slowly made their way down to the river bank, all except Miss Marjorie. Feeling jovial, Miss Marjorie decided to take a shortcut down the steep hill in her brand-new white flip-flops. Carefree and enjoying the beautiful weather, she slowly inched her way down the hill.

Nancy Jo was in the kitchen when she heard Miss Marjorie scream. "Help! I think I broke something!"

Nancy Jo looked out the window and saw Miss Marjorie resting on the hill. The poor dear lady had taken a tumble! She had slipped on a fresh pile of dog poop.

Ranger quickly responded and carried Miss Marjorie up the hill and back into the cottage. "Don't worry, I got you," said Ranger. "Thankfully, you're not very heavy."

Nancy Jo opened the sliding glass door for them and Ranger set her down in an overstuffed chair.

"I thought you picked up all the dog poop" Ranger said to Nancy Jo.

"I did pick it up," said Nancy Jo, "but I think Biscuit just pooped a fresh pile"

"Oh, brother" Ranger responded. "Go get me some ice"

Ranger propped Miss Marjorie's foot up. It was beginning to swell like a balloon. "I'm sorry about this," said Ranger.

Miss Marjorie was a happy-go-lucky gal, and even though it felt like there was a bone broken in her foot, she remained upbeat.

"Here," said Ranger, handing Miss Marjorie a bag of ice wrapped in a dish towel. "Put this on it."

Miss Marjorie was in pain, but Ranger waiting on her hand and foot somehow made her feel better. *He sure makes a cute nurse*, she thought. She knew he still missed Lila but couldn't help thinking, m*aybe he needs a special lady in his life again. Someone like me!*

Meanwhile, the pastor stood in the river. The shallow area of the river had a sandy bottom which was perfect for baptisms. Unaware of the dog poop accident, the pastor proceeded. "All who wish to make a public display of their faith are welcome to come into the waters of baptism."

A young man joined the pastor in the river, ready for his baptism. The pastor declared, "Like Jesus who died, was buried and rose again, your sins will be buried and you will receive the cutting away of the old sinful nature and arise to walk in newness of life. I baptize you in the name of the Lord." The Pastor then immersed him under water and then went on to baptize a family of five, dunking them in the river one at a time.

After the baptisms, a big guy named Bo kindly helped Miss Marjorie hobble out to the driveway and drove her home. The rest of the church people stayed and enjoyed kayaking and fishing. The curious kids went to the hen house eager to see the backyard flock. The spoiled chickens and ducks, overdue for snacks, pulled at the kids' clothes and looked for hidden treats. But they didn't find any until Nancy Jo showed up with a bag of Cheerios. "I knew they would be pestering you," she said. "They don't like missing snack time." While the flock gobbled up the Cheerios, the few remaining families relaxed, sprawled out on the deck furniture. They soaked up the peaceful scenic views, and enjoyed lighthearted conversation. As evening neared everyone cleared out and headed home.

The Growing Trio

A few days had passed and Cornflake was still adjusting to being just a regular chicken again. She longed for the day she could visit Sippy, Dippy, and Damp at Green Pastures. Nancy Jo said she would take her there to visit. She promised.

Today Rhubarb and Dumplin finally joined the outside flock. They had been kept inside a dog crate for several days, inside the chicken run. Nancy Jo opened the crate door for Rhubarb and Dumplin, and they ran to hide from the others at first, finding whatever they could find to hide behind.

When Rhubarb got up the nerve to belly up to the feeder,

Cookie scolded her. "Get away Newbie!"

Rhubarb ran and hid behind a shovel for a while, but she was really hungry, so she made another dash for the feeder.

"Get lost," chided Penelope. "We don't like new peeps!"

Scared, Rhubarb darted and hid behind a feed bucket. Dumplin, who was trying to look invisible facing the corner, was frightened too and her stomach was rumbling so loudly that even Butterscotch could hear its noisy growls. Things were not going well for Rhubarb and Dumplin!

Insightful Butterscotch hopped up to perch on a high roosting bar. "May I have everyone's attention?" Butterscotch spoke with authority and continued. "My mom repeated this quote to me since I was a baby hatchling and I think it bears repeating now. 'In everything, do unto others as you would have them do unto you.'"

After hearing Butterscotch's words, Cookie and Penelope knew they were wrong for treating Rhubarb and Dumplin so badly, and they were sorry. Cookie and Penelope made their way to Rhubarb, still hiding behind the feed bucket. "You can eat as much as you want, and Dumplin too," they said.

Rhubarb and Dumplin felt greatly relieved. They made a beeline for the feeder and ate their fill of chicken feed crumbles. Thanks to sensible Butterscotch, things were peaceful in the chicken run again. Butterscotch, full of wisdom, was not the head chicken for nothing!

As Rhubarb and Dumplin felt more comfortable in the run, Dumplin managed to jump onto the wobbly new chicken swing. Shaky at first, she got her balance and began to swing back and forth on the swing. "Weeeeeeeeee!" shrieked Dumplin with delight. Soon she was bravely swinging high, gliding back and forth. "I'm flying!" she shrieked.

After they saw how much fun Dumplin was having, the other hens wanted to give the swing a try too. Butterscotch took a turn on the swing. She enjoyed it too, but with her full-figured body the swing didn't budge too easily. The chicken sisters broke out into loud cackles as Butterscotch managed to gain momentum only to move the swing a few inches or so, but at least she was able to sway back and forth a wee bit. They all took turns swinging on the swing, seeing who could swing the highest until the sun began to set.

The fall days were much shorter now and it turned unseasonably cold. It was beginning to feel more like winter. Though the cold wind couldn't cut through Twinkie and Pancake's coats of thick down feathers, the chicken sisters found huddling in the hen house to be much cozier than hanging out in the frigid air.

As the chilly wind whipped through the run, Cornflake decided to go to bed early. "Burr!" she cried. "I'm going to my warm roost." She was always the first one to the roost. Sleep was very important to her, and she appreciated her familiar cushy roost.

Dusk moved in. Butterscotch, Penelope, Cookie, Dumplin and Rhubarb had a hard time seeing in the dim light, so one by one they walked up the narrow ramp to join Cornflake for the night. Just as Rhubarb entered the roost, the flock was startled by a sinister high-pitched scream coming from the woods.

"What's that?" asked Rhubarb, with her eyes wide open.

"Oh, don't worry," said Butterscotch. "That's just Vixen the fox. She likes to scare us with her screams, but we're safe in here."

Snuggled tight together for warmth, the chicken sisters felt safe and comfortable even as Vixen's haunting screams seemed to surround them. As they nestled together, they sleepily listened to her loud wild screams, but after she carried on for a while her screams began to grow faint and at last faded into the night. The chicken sisters and ducks could barely keep their eyes open. Soon they were all sleeping like babies.

12

Fall Flurries

Twinkie And Pancake

It had only been five days since Cornflake was separated from Sippy, Dippy, and Damp, but it seemed much longer. She missed them more and more each day. Nancy Jo had taped a couple of photos inside Cornflake's roost of Cornflake and her brood on the last day they were at Cork Pine Cottage. Sippy, Dippy, and Damp looked content and the sun was shining. But now the skies looked bleak and light snow flurries swirled in the cold wind.

Bill from Green Pastures had phoned Nancy Jo today and told her how the kids were entertained by watching the ducks play. He said they were especially tickled with Sippy, Dippy, and Damp because they were so comical!

Sippy and Dippy had formed an unlikely friendship with Marmalade, a fat orange cat. Bill said it was *so* funny to see them waddling at full speed, chasing the cat! They loved to cuddle with her, nap with her, and of course, sample her cat food. Damp had become quite the hit with the lady ducks and his shameless flirting kept everyone in stitches. The daily dose of lighthearted chuckles was like a healing medicine to the troubled kids.

Cornflake looked at the photos with longing and tears welled up in her eyes. She knew her beloved babies were in good hands, and she truly was thankful they were independent and happy, but today their absence seemed unbearable. She missed mothering them, and her heart felt sad and heavy like an anchor. Cornflake had hit an all-time low. She felt lost and desperate. She had to do something!

She turned to her chicken sisters. "I need all your eggs!"

"Oh no. Are you thinking of sitting on our eggs?" asked Penelope.

"Yes, I am!" answered Cornflake.

113

"The poster chicken of *all* sitting hens is at it again," sighed Penelope.

"Can you *please* just hand over your egg?" asked Cornflake.

Reluctantly, Penelope complied and surrendered her egg. Cornflake needed as many eggs as she could get in order to up her chances at hatching baby chicks. Rhubarb and Dumplin, still too young, hadn't started laying eggs yet. That only left three more eggs from Butterscotch, Cookie, and Twinkie.

"Pardon me," said Cornflake politely as she lifted up Cookie's wing and scooped up her egg while she was still laying on it.

"Hey, you're getting waaaay too personal!" squawked Cookie. "Get a grip!"

Cornflake blushed, but she *had* to have that egg!

Butterscotch, knowing her egg was next in demand, looked concerned. "Cornflake, I know your heart is sad right now, but I'm not sure if this is the answer to your problems. I still don't understand how it worked out for you the first time, but surely it won't work a second time. Here you can have my egg."

"Thank you, Butterscotch. I'll take good care of it," said Cornflake as her eyes landed on Twinkie who had her head tucked under her wing and was sleeping soundly. "Maybe I can snatch her egg," whispered Cornflake to herself as she edged closer.

"What *are* you doing?" scolded Penelope. Twinkie still half asleep began to stir.

"I need her egg!" said Cornflake. "She doesn't care about her eggs anyway."

"Does she know you hatched *her* eggs?" blurted Penelope just as Twinkie's eyes popped open. "Maybe she would care!"

"What are you talking about?" asked Cornflake.

"I thought you knew Nancy Jo swapped your eggs with

114

Twinkie's," said Penelope. "During the summer, when the neighbor lady was visiting, I heard her and Nancy Jo talking about it."

Shaken by the news, Cornflake cried out. "You mean my chickens are ducks? Twinkie's ducks?"

Twinkie, who was silently listening, sprang to her feet. "I *KNEW* it! Those babies of yours are *MINE* and *NO* you are not taking my egg. How dare you hatch my eggs!"

The shocking truth crushed Cornflake, but now as the truth sank in, she suddenly understood why her chickens seemed so different and how they loved to swim. They did look a little different from her too. Now it all made sense. Yes, they were ducks and not only ducks, but Twinkie's ducks! Cornflake had no doubt that Penelope was being honest with her. The painful truth was eye-opening, and she needed to go to her roost and think about things.

The truth was eye-opening for Twinkie too. Thinking back, Twinkie recalled how Sippy, Dippy, and Damp looked familiar to her, and then she spouted off to her flock mates. "I *knew* there was a family resemblance. They look just like me!" boasted Twinkie. "*I'M* the real mom here! Cornflake is a fake mom!" squawked Twinkie.

"What is going on around here?" asked Butterscotch.

"Cornflake hatched *MY* eggs. That's what's going on around here!" snapped Twinkie.

"Pipe down!" scolded Butterscotch. "Cornflake loves those babies, even if they *were* hatched from your eggs. Show some respect!"

Twinkie listened to Butterscotch and piped down, but she had a hard time keeping her ever flapping bill shut. The sweet silence didn't last though because she just *had* to quack the news at full volume to her poor flock mates as well as the neighbors. "I'm a mom! I'm a mom to Sippy, Dippy, and Damp!

Twinkie enjoyed rubbing salt into Cornflake's wounds. "She deserved it," she told herself. After all, Cornflake was *not* the *real* mom. *She was.*

Pancake

13

Too Many Moms

Backyard Fun

Twinkie continued with her downright hurtful remarks. "Cornflake isn't a real mom! I'm the mom to those ducks!" Her loud, irritating taunts forced Cornflake to stay holed up inside her roost. Twinkie's high-pitched voice pierced through the thin walls. There was no escape.

Cornflake gazed at the photos of Sippy, Dippy, and Damp with new eyes. Now she could see how they really did resemble Twinkie, but in her heart, she still loved them like her own. In fact, she simply adored them. In her heart they would always be *her* babies.

The flock had enough of Twinkie's ranting. Butterscotch found a strand of loose baling twine from a bale of straw and got an idea. She waited until Twinkie dozed off then tied the string around her bill. "That should do the trick," said Butterscotch as Pancake and the chicken sisters gathered around Twinkie and looked on in amazement.

Surrounded by her flock mates, Twinkie woke up, startled to see so many eyes looking at her. She tried to quack but no sound came out. She couldn't open her bill! Twinkie stretched her neck and made a crazy face as she strained to see her bill. But she couldn't see the string tied around it. Twinkie struggled to quack and was starting to panic when Pancake came to her side.

"You'll be okay, Twinkie," reassured Pancake. Pancake's soothing voice calmed Twinkie. She looked at him and questioned him with her eyes.

Butterscotch then confronted Twinkie. "You have been unkind to Cornflake and you have been hard to live with. If you promise to quit being a twit, I will remove the string I tied around your bill. Do you promise to behave?"

Twinkie nodded. Butterscotch untied the string and freed Twinkie's bill, and Twinkie kept remarkably quiet as Pancake comforted her.

Just as things calmed down, Nancy Jo came down to the hen

house. She carried a rake and wore her handy chicken print apron which had pockets for egg collecting. Like usual, she was singing and Cornflake was relieved to hear her voice.

Nancy Jo greeted her flock with a made-up tune. "I got the cutest little babies . . . I got the cutest little baaaaabbbies, I got the cutest little babies in all of the world!"

Looking for treats, the spoiled hens minus Cornflake, ran to her followed by Twinkie and Pancake. "I'm here to clean out this pigsty not give you treats," teased Nancy Jo. She raked the old bedding out of the bottom of the hen house where Twinkie and Pancake slept and replaced it with fresh pine shavings. After tidying up the run with a brisk raking she finally opened the box of Cheerios.

Nancy Jo had the flock eating Cheerios out of her hand when she noticed Cornflake was not with the others. Concerned, Nancy Jo went to check the roost for Cornflake and found her there looking awful and like she had been crying.

"What's wrong Cornflake?" asked Nancy Jo.

Cornflake blubbered, "I know you swapped my eggs and so does Twinkie. She says I'm not a real mom!"

"You are a real mom," said Nancy Jo. "Twinkie is too impatient to hatch an egg. I don't think she knows how to be a mom. Don't worry, I have good news! Sippy, Dippy, and Damp are coming here on Saturday to visit you. Everything is already arranged."

Cornflake cheered up. "Yay, they're coming to Cork Pine Cottage!" she shouted.

Nancy Jo refilled the nesting boxes with fresh pine shavings and threw Cornflake some Cheerios. "Don't worry that little feathered head," she said with a smile. "I have to go help Ranger unload a truckload of firewood, but I'll be back."

Cornflake still felt uncomfortable around Twinkie, so stayed in her roost. As she settled into her fresh, sweet smelling pine shavings she remembered her egg hatching plan. Doing what she knew best, she gathered up her sisters' eggs as well as two of her own that she had stashed, and stacked them into a neat pile. She told herself she would just have to start all over again. She would hatch new babies and show Twinkie she was a real mom after all!

It was Saturday, and just as Nancy Jo had promised, Sippy, Dippy, and Damp arrived for a visit. They ran to the hen house excited to see their mom. Happy clucks and quacks filled the backyard! Cornflake beamed with joy as Twinkie shot her a frosty look. The sibling ducks were surprised to see the hen house all redecorated.

"The hen house looks so different!" said Dippy.

"Kinda girly but nice!" remarked Damp.

"I like it!" Sippy chimed in.

The ducks were thrilled to be back at Cork Pine Cottage, and it was just like old times Playful squirrels zipped up and down nearby trees and watched Sippy, Dippy, and Damp play games of Hide-and-Seek and tag with their mom. The ground was now a deep carpet of dead leaves and made crunching sounds as they waded through them, followed Cornflake, and scratched in the dirt.

As the afternoon wore on Cornflake finally got up the nerve to tell her precious babies about their biological mom, Ms. Twinkie. "I have something to tell you," said Cornflake. "I hope it won't upset you, but when I hatched you, the eggs weren't mine. They were Twinkie's. Twinkie is your biological mom."

Sippy, Dippy, and Damp's eyes widened and their bills dropped open at first, but as they looked at Cornflake, the only mom they had ever known, they could see the worry on her face. Sippy gave Cornflake one of the biggest squeeziest hugs in the history of hugs! She hugged her so hard Cornflake could barely breathe!

"Oh, Mom, you *are* our real mom, Twinkie's eggs or not!" said Damp, and they all agreed.

Cornflake cried tears of gratefulness. *All that worrying for nothing*, she thought. Her babies loved her like their real mom because she was a real mom!

Cornflake led Sippy, Dippy, and Damp near the run, so they could get closer to Twinkie who was feasting on warm oatmeal. "Excuse me, Ms. Twinkie," said Damp. "We would like to thank you for your eggs that you let our mom hatch. We wouldn't be here without you."

"Yeah, yeah, you're welcome," answered Twinkie between big slurps of oatmeal. "Now if you don't mind, I have to eat this oatmeal before it gets cold. Ta ta!" After brushing off her ducks, Twinkie continued to slurp her food eating more like a pig than a duck. Twinkie didn't seem to give a fig about being a real mom to her biological babies. After all, she had more important things to tend to, like warm oatmeal.

Unruffled by Twinkie's rude dismissal, Sippy, Dippy, and Damp realized their biological mom was just that, but they didn't hold it against her. The ducks were thankful to have a mom like Cornflake. She had a true mother's heart.

Cornflake was not surprised by Twinkie's behavior. She didn't have that devoted mom instinct thing. Twinkie was just being Twinkie. Cornflake felt so much lighter now that the truth was out in the open. "Let's play!" she shouted.

Cornflake and her brood of ducks played hard that day until it was time for Ranger to take them back to Green Pastures. At dusk, Cornflake walked up the ramp to her beloved roost. She had so much fun with her family! She felt confident knowing she was a real mom. She no longer needed to prove anything to Twinkie, herself, or anybody! She looked at her pile of eggs. *Oh, what the heck! I may as well hatch these perfectly good eggs!* she thought. She carefully perched herself on her nest and settled in for the night. It was time to get some much-needed shut-eye.

Nancy Jo picked up the ringing house phone. "Hi, Grandma! Yes, we're doing okay. Dad ran to the General Store to pick up a pizza for dinner."

"Oh, okay," said Grandma. "I was wondering if it would be okay if we came and visited tomorrow? Uncle Robby flew in from Wisconsin and will only be here for a couple days."

"Sure, Grandma. Maybe we can do some baking."

"Of course, we will," said Grandma who shared Nancy Jo's love for baking. "I have a great recipe for Old Fashioned Sorghum Cookies, but I ran out of sorghum."

"Maybe Ranger can pick some up at the General Store," said Nancy Jo. "I'll text him right now before he leaves the store. Okay, I will see you tomorrow!"

Nancy Jo texted Ranger and caught him before he left the store. He looked for sorghum but didn't see any. As he was leaving the store, he spotted Miss Marjorie. His heart sank as he saw she was using an orthopedic knee scooter to get around.

"Hi, Marjorie," he said. "How's the foot?"

"Well, it's been a challenge, but I'm doing okay."

Ranger felt somewhat to blame for Marjorie's injury. *I should have double-checked for dog poop*, he thought. Then he asked, "Do you know any place that sells sorghum? I don't know what it is exactly, but it's used in baking and my mom needs it. She's visiting tomorrow."

"I've heard of sorghum," said Miss Marjorie, "but I've never actually tasted it. You need to go to a larger store, like the Piggly Wiggly, or I'm sure you could order it online. But if she's coming tomorrow, that won't work."

"Okay," said Ranger. "I guess I'll have to go on a sorghum run. How did you get here? Did you drive?"

"No, I can't drive," said Miss Marjorie. "That's my niece over there in the Chevy. She brought me up here to pick up some bread and milk."

"Want to go on a sorghum run with me?" asked Ranger. "I've got pizza!"

"Okay, you talked me into it!" Marjorie willingly agreed to the idea. A little "Ranger time" sounded good to her!

Ranger helped Miss Marjorie into the passenger seat of his pick up and put the knee scooter in the truck bed. Two of Ranger's dogs, Tucker, the Australian Shepherd and Eddie, the oversized yellow lab, were in the back seat, wagging their tails. They were eager to greet the nice lady with their wet noses which were instantly alerted to the smell of something delicious! The whiff of spicy pizza sauce and the savory baked crust smelled heavenly to the dogs, and its intoxicating aroma was also calling out to Ranger's empty growling stomach.

As they headed to the Piggly Wiggly, Ranger called Nancy Jo. "I won't be home right away. I'm making a sorghum run with Miss Marjorie."

"You're with Miss Marjorie?" Nancy Jo was surprised, but she held her tongue and just said "okay" and hung up. Nancy Jo didn't like the idea of her dad out cruising around with Miss Marjorie. It didn't set well with her. Her dad was not on the market for a girlfriend!

As Ranger drove, he turned to Marjorie, "How about we have

some of that pizza now. Do you mind handing me a slice?"

"Here you go," said Marjorie and handed Ranger a piping hot slice. "I don't see any napkins, but here's a roll of toilet paper you could use."

Ranger laughed. "Perfect!" They had to drive to another county to get to the Piggly Wiggly. Miss Marjorie scrunched her nose as she observed the cyclone of dog hair blowing around the truck cab and the matted dog hair that was stuck to the upholstery. Ranger couldn't help but notice Marjorie's disgust.

"This is the dog's truck," Ranger explained. "I'm just the driver. My older lab, Biscuit, used to love to come along too, but lately he just wants to stay home."

"Oh, I understand," said Miss Marjorie respectfully, trying to ignore the flying dog hair. "I may as well have some pizza too. I *am* a little hungry." Miss Marjorie grabbed a slice, though she had to close her eyes while she ate, to avoid seeing the "freedom festival" of hair!

Between the two of them they ate almost the whole pizza. They threw the dogs the chewy crusts or "pizza bones" as Ranger called them. When they finally got to the Piggly Wiggly Ranger ran in by himself to look for sorghum. He looked up and down the baking aisle and even asked a clerk for help, but she didn't think they carried it. Ranger picked up two kinds of molasses instead, some black strap molasses and a sugar cane molasses since the clerk told him they could be used in place of sorghum. Ranger then then dropped Miss Marjorie off at her house and headed home.

Back at the cottage, Nancy Jo made her own dinner, a fluffernutter sandwich: peanut butter with a thick layer of marshmallow creme. When Ranger showed up with two cold shriveled slices of leftover pizza and molasses, Nancy Jo told Ranger that Uncle Robby, Ranger's brother, would be visiting.

"Oh, Robby's coming too?" said Ranger. "Maybe I better barbecue a nice pork shoulder for pulled pork tomorrow." Both Ranger and Uncle Robby loved all pork products. Nancy Jo had nicknamed them "The Pork Brothers." They never met a pork chop they didn't like! Uncle Robby was a caring, skilled veterinarian who worked a lot, but he enjoyed working with animals.

As dusk fell Nancy Jo pulled on her muck boots and hurried to the backyard to secure the hen house. The whole flock was sound asleep already except Pancake and Twinkie. They liked to stay up late and chit chat at the water bowl, and they preferred sleeping in short spurts. Pancake had the amazing ability to sleep with one eye open, always guarding Twinkie, even in the middle of the night.

"Goodnight," said Nancy Jo as she threw them some iceberg lettuce.

Skipper

Biscuit, Tucker, and Eddie barked uncontrollably and rushed to the front door in a stampede. The doorbell always rustled them up from their usual vegetative state. The Kimball's had arrived: Grandma, Gramps, Skipper, their little Boston Terrier, and Uncle Robby. There was a lot of commotion with four excited dogs, but the dogs loved company and their little dog cousin.

Nancy Jo flung open the front door. "Hi, Grandma, Gramps, and Uncle Robby. Come on in!" They all piled in with their overnight bags. Nancy Jo noticed Gramps' looked a bit wilted from the long drive. He was just tired and hungry but was really glad they had made it in one piece.

"I'll put on a pot of coffee as soon as I put all these dogs outside," said Ranger.

"I brought some pastries to go with," said Uncle Robby.

Grandma fed Skipper his "little dog" kibble out of Skipper's own tiny bowl from home. Then she put Skipper outside to play with the other dogs.

"Where's Cal?" Grandma asked Nancy Jo.

"He's at his friend's, Wyatt's house, but he'll be home later," said Nancy Jo.

"Okay," said Grandma. "Are you ready to bake?"

"Yes, Grandma," said Nancy Jo. "Let's bake!"

"Did Ranger pick up the sorghum?" Grandma asked.

"No," answered Nancy Jo. "He and Miss Marjorie went to the store together, but the store didn't have sorghum, so he brought home two kinds of molasses instead."

"Oh?" Grandma raised her eyebrows. "That is a juicy bit of news! Is Ranger interested in Miss Marjorie?"

"I hope not!" said Nancy Jo as her face tensed up and her eyes widened. "He doesn't need a girlfriend!"

Grandma sensed she hit a nerve and changed the subject. "Well, what do you want to bake?"

"We have lots of molasses now," said Nancy Jo, "so maybe some ginger snaps?"

"Okay, we'll make ginger snaps," said Grandma. "I stopped at the fruit market on the way here and picked up some apples, so we can also make an apple pie."

"I want to make cow pies too!" said Nancy Jo.

"What are cow pies?" asked Grandma. "They sound terrible!"

"They're no bake cookies with oats, cocoa, and peanut butter. We call 'em cow pies."

"Oh! Okay, now I know what you mean," said Grandma. "Those are a classic! Well, we better get to it!"

As Nancy Jo and Grandma got to their baking, Ranger set up a table in the living room for the guys to play cards while Uncle Robby guzzled massive amounts of strong coffee. Gramps, also branded with the handle "the white tornado" by the family, relaxed and changed into his very neat and tidy casual clothes. His trademark gleaming white tennis shoes and blinding white socks were legendary.

Gramps was anticipating a long overdue euchre game with the boys. Euchre was a Kimball tradition, except there was a problem. Since Cal wasn't home, they were short a player.

Just then the phone rang. Ranger picked it up in the living room. "Oh, Hi, Marjorie. No, I didn't see any keys, but hold on and I'll check my truck."

Ranger set the phone down and ran outside. After a few minutes he returned. "I found them!" Before he hung up, he said, "Yeah, no problem we'll be home."

"Who's Marjorie?" asked Gramps. "Is she your girlfriend?"

"No," said Ranger. "She's a lady from church, and we're just friends."

"Does she play euchre?" asked Gramps.

"I don't really know, but I guess I could ask her," said Ranger. "You guys ready for some pulled pork sandwiches yet?"

Ranger set up a couple of folding TV tray tables in the living room and loaded them up with food. You could have heard a pin drop in the living room as the three men dug into the tall stack of tender barbecue pulled pork sandwiches, kettle chips, creamy homemade coleslaw, raspberry Jell-O, and of course, baked beans and sweet tea.

14

Out of the Blue

Tucker And Eddie

Nancy Jo bristled when she heard Miss Marjorie's voice coming from the living room. Ranger came into the kitchen and grabbed Marjorie's keys off the counter. "What's she doing here?" Nancy Jo asked.

"She's after these," Ranger said as he dangled the keys in front of her and dashed out of the room.

"Of course, she just happens to show up everywhere Ranger happens to be," Nancy Jo muttered under her breath to her grandma.

"She's just here to pick up her keys," reassured Grandma.

"No, I think she's here to pick up something else!" snapped Nancy Jo. Unable to bottle up her intense emotions, Nancy Jo rolled her eyes and breathed out a long frustrated groan. "Well, I'm sick of Miss Marjorie!" she vented to her Grandma.

"Just ignore her, dear, and finish making those cow pies," said Grandma with a wink, trying her best to lighten the mood as she observed Nancy Jo's smoldering eyes and flushed face.

Nancy Jo stayed quiet and kept her ears open to hear the conversation in the living room. Gramps, hopeful to actually start playing euchre, asked Marjorie, "Do you play euchre?"

"I used to play a lot, but I haven't played in a long time," answered Marjorie.

"Do you wanna play with us?" Gramps asked her. "Please? We need another player."

"Well, sure!" Marjorie replied cheerfully. "I'll give it a go. I just have to run out and tell my niece who's waiting for me in the driveway." Marjorie left and came back. "Now, who's my partner?"

Nancy Jo was within earshot and burst into the living room to try to control the situation that, in her eyes, was out of control. "Miss Marjorie, meet my Uncle Robby, your handsome

133

euchre partner. Did I mention he's also a very successful eligible bachelor?"

Miss Marjorie smiled awkwardly. "Hello, Robby. I guess we're partners."

Nancy Jo slipped back into the kitchen, pleased with her ploy to throw Miss Marjorie's hound dog nose off Ranger's scent. She stirred her batch of cow pies over the stove burner and brought them to a boil. After they thickened, she plopped gooey spoonfuls of the warm mixture onto wax paper to cool and harden.

As Nancy Jo peeled apples, Grandma rolled out the pie crust to line the bottom of the pie plate. Grandma whispered to her, "Try not to worry too much about your dad. You know he loved your mom, and he always will."

"Yeah, I know," sighed Nancy Jo. "Do you mind if I take a little break and check on my flock?"

"Go ahead, dear. I'll finish up."

Nancy Jo darted past the living room undetected by the others who were still absorbed in their euchre game. She was surprised to find herself so angry at Miss Marjorie. She used to love Miss Marjorie's loud bubbly giggles, but now as her hearty belly laughs bellowed from the living room, Nancy Jo could almost feel smoke coming out of her ears!

In the mud room she slipped on her coat and boots. As she made her way past the living room for the second time, Uncle Robby called out, "Hey, where you going?"

"I'm just going to the backyard for a bit," replied Nancy Jo.

Uncle Robby nodded. "Oh, okay. Oh, wait a minute, you just reminded me! Hold on. I have something for your chickens."

Nancy Jo waited as Uncle Robby went to the guest room to rifle through his things. When he returned, he held out a crumpled brown paper bag to her. "Here you go. A lady who comes to my vet clinic makes these, so I had her make some for you."

Nancy Jo pulled out some unusually shaped pieces of colorful printed fabric. "What are these?" she asked.

"They're chicken diapers," Uncle Robby informed her.

"Oh, I've heard of chicken diapers," said Nancy Jo, "but I've never actually seen one before. I can't wait to try these! I think my chickens will love wearing them. Thank you, Uncle Robby."

"You're welcome, Nancy Jo. Enjoy!"

Nancy Jo felt a great lift in her mood as she headed to the backyard. Grandma, meanwhile, cut strips of pie pastry with a pizza cutter and formed a perfect lattice top crust for the apple pie. Then she put it in the oven to bake. All the while the euchre game was going strong. Gramps and Ranger were winning.

Nancy Jo kept two plastic containers full of water near the back door of the cottage. They were old plastic cat litter containers with handles and held roughly four gallons of water each. Nancy Jo had to lug the heavy water out to the backyard run and refill the flock's big water bowl with fresh water twice a day. This was the hard part in caring for the flock. Since the nighttime temperatures were now falling below freezing, the outside water had to be turned off and fresh water had to be carried outside.

Nancy Jo huffed and puffed as the heavy containers of water pulled hard on her arms. Finally, she made her way into the run with a heavy container in each hand. "Hello everyone! How are my good girls and one good boy doing?"

The flock, happy to see her, quacked and clucked "hello" and scurried to gather around her feet. Nancy Jo refilled their food and water and then collected a few chicken eggs. The flock, always greedy for treats, expected a round of delicious snacks. Being as patient as they possibly could, they waited.

When Nancy Jo bent over to pet Butterscotch, Rhubarb jumped onto her back, clucking sweetly. Rhubarb just wanted to snuggle with Nancy Jo in her own odd way. Still hunched over with Rhubarb on her back, Nancy Jo reached for the box of Cheerios. "Don't worry, I didn't forget your snacks. Here you go!"

As the flock munched on Cheerios and cracked corn, Nancy Jo ran back into the cottage and grabbed the bag of chicken diapers. "I'm back," she said as she entered the run. "I want you girls to try these on. Who wants to go first?"

The diapers were printed with fun, colorful patterns. She grabbed one out of the bag that was light blue with yellow daisies. "Hmm, I wonder who would look good in this one?" she said as she studied the chicken sisters.

They looked back at her gullibly, unsure what Nancy Jo was up to.

Nancy Jo scooped up Penelope and gave her a little snuggle. Then she got to work putting on the diaper. Nancy Jo struggled to put it on. "This doesn't look right," she said as poor Penelope looked like she was being strangled by the straps. But like all of Nancy Jo's chickens, Penelope trusted Nancy Jo and calmly let Nancy Jo wriggle with the diaper until she got it to fit just right. "Okay, there you go, Penelope. It fits like a glove."

Penelope stood up tall, with her head held high, proud to wear her pretty new diaper. The fun splash of color against her white feathers made her look indoor party ready!

Nancy Jo picked out a funky purple tie-dyed diaper and put it on Rhubarb. "I'm getting better at this," Nancy Jo said confidently. "It fits perfectly!" She then picked out a red paisley diaper for Butterscotch. Chubby Butterscotch was very patient as Nancy Jo stuffed her into her diaper. It was a bit tight, but Nancy Jo thought she looked sophisticated in it.

Butterscotch didn't feel sophisticated as she lost her balance and fell over beak first in her cute little diaper. "Help!" clucked Butterscotch. Looking red in the cheeks, Butterscotch quickly scrambled to her feet. She fluffed up her feathers and tried to look dignified. It was her duty to uphold her strong image as top chicken, and she couldn't allow herself to be seen as a weak peep.

"Awww Butterscotch, you'll get used to it. Being a chicken fashionista does have a downside." Nancy Jo then went on to fit each hen in a colorful diaper though she practically had to pry Cornflake off her precious collection of eggs. "C'mon Cornflake," pleaded Nancy Jo. "You need a snazzy diaper too. This won't take very long and you can come right back to your eggs."

Cornflake looked like a doll in her pink polka dot diaper. All the hens, new to wearing diapers, now walked like chickens trying to walk in high heels for the first time. The added weight seemed to throw off their balance. Dumplin fell on her side clumsily and refused to stand up. "I'm done, I can't do this!" she clucked firmly.

"Dumplin, please try to get up," coaxed Nancy Jo.

"I'm on a break," said Dumplin flatly.

Knowing Dumplin's weakness for Cheerios, Nancy Jo threw a handful just beyond her beak, and in two shakes and a wink, the tempting Cheerios spurred Dumplin to her feet.

"Okay, girls, we're going to a party!" Nancy Jo unlatched the bottom Dutch door to the run and let the hens out. They wobbled behind her into the cottage and looked leak proof in their snappy nappies. Once inside, the hens followed Nancy Jo upstairs to the main living area. The wide-eyed hens had forgotten what it was like to be indoors. They clucked with ease among themselves until they saw the cottage was full of strange new faces. Shocked to see so many people, the clucking chicken sisters froze mid cluck.

The Kimballs as well as Miss Marjorie were just as shocked to see six chickens in diapers huddled in the living room.

"They look great in their diapers!" said Uncle Robby.

"They look scared," said Ranger.

"They're just a little shy at first," said Nancy Jo.

Miss Marjorie picked up Dumplin and set her in her lap as they played another round of euchre. Dumplin relaxed and stretched out comfortably on Miss Marjorie's lap. She always adored a warm lap. The other hens, sensing no danger, relaxed too and curiously began to explore as everyone went back to what they were doing.

The cottage was strangely quiet except for the light scritch scratch sound of chicken feet moving across the wood floor. Like little cherubs, the hens were so well-behaved! Cornflake followed Nancy Jo into the kitchen. The aroma of sweet-smelling apple pie and spicy ginger snaps swirled in the air as they cooled on the kitchen table.

Cornflake sweetly perched atop a little wooden chair by the kitchen window and enjoyed the new indoor sights and sounds and just being in the kitchen near Nancy Jo. Cornflake clucked contentedly, minding her own business, when out of the blue the cottage shook with the thundering sound of sixteen pounding paws! It was Biscuit, Eddie, Tucker and Skipper!

Cal had returned home and let all the dogs in at once. The

rowdy herd of dogs, startled to see the cottage full of chickens, ran after them with delight. The alarmed chickens squawked, and a flurry of feathers blew around as the surprised hens scattered in a panic. Eddie, the bus sized yellow lab, chased Penelope into the kitchen where she air lifted herself onto the counter and landed on the wax paper filled with rows of cooled cow pies. Seconds later, Cornflake joined her.

The dogs barked hysterically as Penelope and Cornflake trampled over the cow pies. They made deep chicken feet imprints in the treats as they nervously danced back and forth on the counter. Biscuit, Tucker, and Skipper rambunctiously cornered Butterscotch, Jellybean, Cookie, and Dumplin in the living room. They barked excitedly and sounded like a pack of hunting dogs. They wanted to play.

The nervous hens didn't think playing with dogs was a good idea at all! Butterscotch made a run for it right through Tucker's legs. She ran into the kitchen with Tucker and Skipper trailing right behind her.

Biscuit

Biscuit kept a playful watch on the four remaining horrified hens in the living room. Biscuit kept up appearances as a protector and fulfilled his canine obligations by barking and wagging his tail, though his heavy breathing sounded raspy and his "old man" bark sounded weak. He was already starting to tire. Much to Biscuit's surprise, his heavy tail thudded against a large bowl of kettle chips and knocked it off one of the TV tray tables. Glorious kettle chips littered the floor, and Biscuit, relieved to take a break, happily cleaned up the windfall of crunchy floor freebies. Being up in years, Biscuit found tasty chips a lot more interesting than chasing chickens.

Poor Butterscotch looked for a place to hide, but she was cornered. She was too heavy to fly up to the kitchen counter and decided to make a U-turn and run back into the living room. Tucker, Eddie, and Skipper trailed behind Butterscotch, and then Skipper's paw caught the leg of one of the food-laden TV tray tables. The TV tray table fell like a domino and knocked down the other TV tray table next to it, catapulting the bowls of coleslaw and baked beans into the air towards Miss Marjorie.

Cal intervened and caught the bowls in midair, but the contents of beans and coleslaw sloshed out. Miss Marjorie's eyes opened *really* wide as she was splatted with the wet mixture of baked beans and coleslaw.

Nancy Jo couldn't help but laugh with a spiteful sense of satisfaction as Miss Marjorie's hair dripped with runny coleslaw dressing and beans.

"Why are all your chickens in the house?" Cal barked, irritated with Nancy Jo.

"They were doing fine until you let all the dogs in!" Nancy Jo replied sharply.

"You crazy chicken tender! snarled Cal.

"Don't be too hard on Nancy Jo, Cal," said Miss Marjorie. "You can't blame a girl for loving her hens!"

Ranger handed Miss Marjorie a roll of paper towels, and she blotted herself off as best she could, all with a smile on her face. Nancy Jo cringed inwardly and thought, *Maybe I've been too hard on Miss Marjorie. She stuck up for me, and here I was smirking while she was being baptized in beans and coleslaw.*

Nancy Jo had always liked Miss Marjorie up until recently. "The problem," Nancy Jo finally had to admit to herself, "isn't Miss Marjorie at all. The problem is me." The harsh truth was that she couldn't bear to see her dad happy with another woman who wasn't her mom. Nancy Jo felt ashamed for her behavior and promised herself to do better.

"I think it's time to call it a night," said Grandma as she stared at the irregularly shaped blobs of Jell-O on the floor. Cal and Uncle Robby put the dogs back outside and Grandma put Skipper back in his crate. Gramps broke out an array of cleaning products and Nancy Jo didn't even mind when Ranger offered to drive Miss Marjorie home. Peace had been restored inside the little cottage and in Nancy Jo's heart.

Nancy Jo crouched on her knees and peeked under the couch where four of her hens were hiding. "You can come out now," she said. The weary chicken sisters ran to Nancy Jo. "Time to go back outside," Nancy Jo called out to Cornflake and Penelope who were still perched on the kitchen counter. The flock, longing for their peaceful backyard and some rest, headed back to the great outdoors and to their beloved "five cluck" hen house.

15

The Mystery

Chicken Sisters

The fall cold snap continued. It was cold for October and felt more like winter now at Cork Pine Cottage. Twinkie and Pancake no longer swam in their stock tank pond and it would stay empty until spring. It was time to get the run prepared for the coming colder months. Ranger helped Nancy Jo wrap the run in clear heavy plastic to provide a barrier to winter's bitter cold wind and snow.

Pancake and Twinkie adjusted to only having a water bowl to play in. The ducks needed clean water they could dip their heads into in order to keep their eyes and sinuses clean and healthy. The deep-water bowl wasn't as fun as the stock tank pond, but it would have to do.

Keeping the water bowl full was a challenge when the ducks splashed half of it out as soon as it was filled. The flock quickly surrounded the new gigantic pecking block Nancy Jo put inside the run as a cold weather treat. Nancy Jo only gave them pecking blocks during the colder seasons. They provided extra nutrients and were great winter boredom busters.

Nancy Jo worked inside the run alongside her beloved hens and ducks. Cornflake used her beak to pull at Nancy Jo's pant leg. "Don't forget to pick me up!" said Cornflake. Nancy Jo scooped her up and held her for a minute, and then Cornflake ran back to the roost to lay on her eggs. Nancy Jo continued with her chores. She piled high the bedding in the hen house with fresh pine shavings for added warmth and cushiness, and then she brought out some old Christmas lights she found in the garage.

Tinkering in the run, Nancy Jo stood on her tiptoes and struggled to drape several strings of lights around the inside roof of the run when Kenny showed up unexpectedly.

"Hi, Nancy Jo! Your dad told me you were back here. My mom sent me to pick up a carton of eggs."

Surprised and with a runny nose from the chilly air, Nancy Jo discreetly reached into her pocket for a tissue and blew her nose as lady like as possible. She knew she didn't look her best.

Her fine hair was wind-blown and flat, and she was wearing Ranger's flannel work coat which drowned her.

"Hi, Kenny!" she said, trying to sound cheerful. "Okay, I'll grab some eggs for you as soon as I hang this last string of lights."

"Why are you hanging Christmas lights?" Kenny asked.

"Oh, I'm adding some lights because it gets dark so early now," answered Nancy Jo. "Want to help me?"

"Sure, I can help," said Kenny.

Nancy Jo giggled as tall Kenny stooped low like he was doing the limbo and came through the bottom half of the Dutch door to the run. He didn't realize the top half of the door opened up as well.

"Here, I'll take those," he said as the flock kept their eyes on him. Kenny hung the lights effortlessly since he was quite a bit taller than Nancy Jo.

Nancy Jo smiled at him. "Thank you, Kenny. I'll get you some eggs." Nancy Jo grabbed her egg collecting apron hanging on a nail inside the run. "Well, I have four eggs in my apron from this morning, but I'm sure I have more in the refrigerator. Let's go inside and see."

Nancy Jo was ready for a break anyway and who better to take a break with? Kenny, of course! Her handsome crush Kenny was visiting her! *Okay, so it was only to pick up eggs,* she thought, *but it was a start!*

Kenny followed Nancy Jo inside the cottage where she gently scrub brushed the fresh eggs in warm soapy water and grabbed eight more eggs from the fridge. "Would you like some hot chocolate?" she asked.

"Sure," said Kenny. As Nancy Jo filled the tea kettle, she felt her heart thumping in her chest. She thought, *Kenny is so handsome and smart, he could have any girl he wants. And he is here. With me!*

Kenny was all smiles. He thought Nancy Jo was pretty, even when she thought she looked a mess. Kenny liked her for her simple country girl charm, and they shared a common interest—a love for animals.

Nancy Jo and Kenny shared lively conversation, mostly about chickens, as they sipped on several mugs of rich hot chocolate heaped with mini marshmallows. By the time Kenny left, it was dark. Nancy Jo went back to the run. "I have a surprise for all of you!" she announced as she plugged in the lights.

"Oh! They're beautiful," squealed Dumplin. One of the strings was chock -full of sizable blue and white stars that twinkled. The cheerful lights brought on a round of happy quacking from Twinkie and Pancake. The hens stared at the lights with wonder. Now they could see clearly, even in the dark! Colorful, twinkling Christmas lights made the backyard feel cozy, and they would brighten up the dark winter nights. The run looked magical!

Cornflake On A Stroll

It had been two weeks since Sippy, Dippy, and Damp visited Cork Pine Cottage. Nancy Jo headed to the front of the cottage with a twenty-pound bag of bird seed and several suet cakes.

She and Ranger loved to watch the wild birds. So many species of birds flocked to the feeders, especially in the cold months. There were many varieties of woodpeckers, but they kept an eye out for the huge "crow sized" Pileated woodpecker. The male Pileated woodpeckers were mostly black with a white stripe on their face and neck along with a flaming red crest. It was always a thrill to see one these giant colorful woodpeckers perched on one of the feeders or pecking at a suet cake.

Nancy Jo then headed to the backyard to fill more feeders and check on her flock. Twinkie and Pancake quacked "hello" and bobbed their heads at her, and the chicken sisters Butterscotch, Penelope, Cookie, Rhubarb, and Dumplin ran to greet her. Of course, Nancy Jo had brought Cheerios with her. She never showed up empty-handed, and she always gave them generous handfuls.

Stubborn Cornflake didn't show up for snack time. She sat on her nest as if she was super glued to her eggs. A bit concerned, Nancy Jo took a peek inside the roost. Cornflake, all fluffed up, was in full mom mode protecting her eggs. Her eyes smiled and sparkled with joy. Nancy Jo hadn't seen Cornflake look so happy since she became a mom for the first time. Nancy Jo wondered why Cornflake looked as if sunshine had flooded her soul. She moved in closer.

"Okay, Cornflake," said Nancy Jo. "What's gotten into you?"

Cornflake lifted her wings slowly and dramatically to reveal two new baby chicks. Nancy Jo couldn't believe her eyes! Clucking with pride, Cornflake enjoyed watching Nancy Jo's face as she showed off her freshly hatched pride and joy.

Nancy Jo had a soft spot for cute baby chicks and sat with Cornflake to admire the new additions to the flock. So delicate and content under their mom's wings, they were totally dependent on her. Nancy Jo marveled at Cornflake's mysterious accomplishment and wondered how Cornflake managed to hatch two baby chicks.

"I picked out names for them already," said Cornflake. "Since they're both girls I will name one Marigold after my mom and will call the other one Pumpkin after my great hen-mother."

"Oh, I love those names!" said Nancy Jo. "Let's tell your chicken sisters the good news." Nancy Jo called the flock inside the roost. They were flabbergasted to see Cornflake with her new baby chicks.

"It's a miracle," cried Penelope as the others stood in awe.

"That's impossible!" exclaimed Butterscotch. "You did it again!"

Cornflake enjoyed all the attention her babies were getting. Her eyes shone bright and she began to cackle. She sounded a bit like a rooster.

"Okay, are you going to tell us how you hatched baby chicks without a rooster?" asked Butterscotch.

"I have a little secret," said Cornflake in a whispered cluck . "Remember when I visited Green Pastures? Well, I met a very handsome Welsummer rooster named Drumstick. He was very friendly to me when I was crying behind the milk house. Then I was surprised with two baby chicks!"

Nancy Jo's lips curled upwards and turned into a smile. She let out a teensy giggle then erupted into a joyful laugh. She found Cornflake's story quite funny. As Nancy Jo and the flock doted on Cornflake's precious baby chicks, Nancy Jo had an idea. "Let's sing Happy Birthday to welcome Marigold and Pumpkin!"

Cornflake, Butterscotch, Penelope, Cookie, Rhubarb, Dumplin, Pancake, and Twinkie all joined in and sang to the new fuzzy bundles of joy. Then Nancy Jo shut the door to the roost to give Cornflake and her babies some privacy and quiet. Nancy Jo brought out fresh apple slices and warm oatmeal to celebrate the occasion. All was well at Cork Pine Cottage.

The next morning Nancy Jo grabbed the pink chicken harness and leash and made her way out to the backyard. "You're all going for a walk today. " She threw down some Cheerios and filled the water bowl and feeder.

Twinkie was so excited she gobbled up her Cheerios even faster than usual.

"Okay, Twinkie, you can go first."

Nancy Jo slipped the soft pink collar over Twinkie's head and then placed the harness part under her belly, squeezing her as she snapped it under her wings. Twinkie was going for a walk!

Twinkie was thrilled to be out on the grass again even though it was covered with brown crunchy leaves. As she walked along the river bank, she was delighted to find a small patch of hearty yellow wildflowers on the river bank that were still in bloom.

Nancy Jo walked Twinkie to her favorite meadow. Twinkie quacked serenely as fond memories of her darling Tickle rushed back to her mind. She could picture him as if it was yesterday, marching proudly, loyally guarding her as she hatched her daily egg. After Twinkie's exhilarating walk, Nancy Jo took Pancake and each of the chicken sisters for their own walking adventure too. They all enjoyed stretching their legs and ambling the glorious rugged backyard.

Cornflake went for a brief stroll and then hurried back to care for her fuzzy baby chicks. She had moved back into the travel crate once again to mother her youngins'. There she would raise them and show them the ropes of chicken life. Against all odds, Cornflake had hatched her *breakfast eggs*. Under her loving wings, she had nurtured both baby chicks and ducklings.

She was the best mother of all mother hens!

Epilogue

The Mother Hen

Just as a nurturing mother hen gathers her chicks under her wings, God yearns to gather you unto Himself. He loves you with a pure, selfless love. I hope you will hear the cry of God's heart and accept His divine invitation to come under the shelter of His loving wings. He graciously offers you the free gift of eternal life. Are you willing to receive it?

"For God so loved the world that He gave His one and only Son, that whoever believes in Him shall not perish but have eternal life." (John 3:16). Jesus gave up His life for your sins so you could live in right standing with God. If you have faith in your heart to believe in God's redeeming love, simply ask Jesus to come and live in your heart. He will.

"Yet to all who did receive Him, to those who believed in His name, He gave the right to become children of God." (John 1:12). He longs for a relationship with you. Life is so much better under the shadow of a loving "Mother Hen." Are you willing to be gathered unto Him? "How often I have longed to gather your children together, as a hen gathers her chicks under her wings, but you were not willing." (Matthew 23:37).

Made in the USA
Columbia, SC
29 November 2022